The Violin Lover

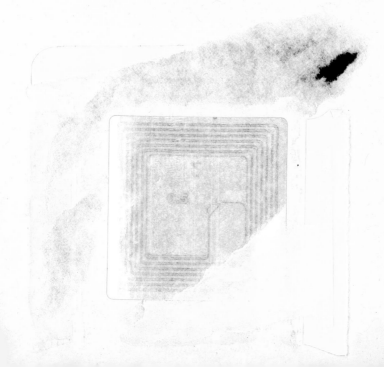

Also by SUSAN GLICKMAN

POETRY
Complicity
The Power to Move
Henry Moore's Sheep and Other Poems
Hide & Seek
Running in Prospect Cemetery: New & Selected Poems

CRITICISM
*The Picturesque & the Sublime: A Poetics of
the Canadian Landscape*

The Violin Lover

SUSAN GLICKMAN

GOOSE LANE

Edited by Lisa Alward and Laurel Boone.
Cover photograph: Stefan Junger, istockphoto.
Cover and interior design by Julie Scriver.
Printed in Canada.
10 9 8 7 6 5 4 3 2 1

Library and Archives Canada Cataloguing in Publication

Glickman, Susan, 1953-
The violin lover / Susan Glickman.

ISBN 0-86492-433-X

I. Title.

PS8563.L49V56 2006   C813'.54   C2005-906433-1

Published with the support of the Canada Council for the Arts and the
New Brunswick Culture and Sport Secretariat. We acknowledge the financial
support of the Government of Canada through the Book Publishing Industry
Development Program (BPDIP) for our publishing activities.

Goose Lane Editions
469 King Street
Fredericton, New Brunswick
CANADA E3B 1E5
www.gooselane.com

for Toan, Jesse and Rachel
and for Anna Wyner
in memory of Uncle Sam Nagley

What do you call
the muscle we long with? Spirit?
I don't think so. Spirit is a far cry. This
is a casting outward which
unwinds inside the chest. A hole
which complements the heart.
The ghost of a chance.

— Don McKay, "Twinflower"

CONTENTS

Autumn – Winter 1934

Spring – Summer 1935

Autumn 1935 – Spring 1936

Coda

Autumn – Winter 1934

A Body

The boys were riding the sphinx when they noticed it, floating down the Thames in a leisurely way. An untidy black bundle, like a poorly rolled rug or a cast-off sofa cushion, partially submerged. The smallest, his knees chapped almost as red as his cheeks, slid off and ran to find a stick, hoping to snag a prize; the other two kept bickering about what it was and where it came from.

Their shrill voices interrupted Dr. Edward Abraham's post-concert reverie as he strolled along the Embankment. Exasperated, he turned up his collar against both the boys and the dank November wind. Ned stroked the fine cashmere appreciatively: it was nice to be warm, and even nicer to be admired. A coat like this helped a lot. It made life easier that women found him attractive and men respected him. A man who was handsome and accomplished needn't justify himself all the time; he had instant credibility and, therefore, freedom.

Oddly enough, a man could be admired for opposite reasons: for standing out, or for fitting in. Ned had done everything he could to fit in, but he still felt conspicuously Semitic, like Cleopatra's Needle, the sphinxes at its feet poor relations to those stately British lions guarding Trafalgar Square. Of course, the obelisk stood out all the more because everything around it fit together so well. To his right stood the Houses of Parliament, burnished gold, exhaling authority; to his left, beyond Waterloo Bridge and veiled by trees, lurked the calm, severe façade of Somerset House, sequestering lesser mysteries and bustling with bureaucrats; and farther north and east shone the dome of St. Paul's, a monk's pate full of whispering. The white city gleamed in the weak November sun, looking as immortal as the Alps and as impervious to time and change.

A bulky man smelling of pipe tobacco jostled his elbow, and Ned realized that more and more people had been gathering on the Embankment.

"I saw it first! I saw it *first!*" the little boy shouted. He'd found a stick and now ran down the north steps to a little sandy beach, briefly uncovered by the tide, to poke at the thing about to wash up there.

"Surely it's a body?" whispered a woman on tiptoe, one baby balanced on her hip and another in the rocking pram she leaned on for support.

"Not likely. It's just some rubbish someone's thrown in the river," replied a well-dressed fellow, folding his newspaper neatly and tucking it under his arm as he peered over for a better view.

"No, look, I swear, those are arms and legs. Look!" said a man in a brown cap.

"Where?"

"It's an old Jew. See the beard?"

"How can you see a beard in that lot? It could be anything — grass, wool, anything. Besides, there's no hat."

"It must have floated away, you idiot."

"Mother of God, have mercy on his soul," muttered a lady in a worn plaid coat, crossing herself. Her meagre mouse-coloured hair was scraped so tightly into a bun that her eyebrows pulled up at the corners.

Sure to give her a headache, Ned thought, as he forced himself forward to have a look. It definitely was a body and had been in the river for some time, to judge by its swollen purple hands. The tides here frequently kept bodies under for days before releasing them; the Thames had always been a temperamental god. Luckily for the increasing press of onlookers, this one floated face down, a long grey beard wafting around it like grim seaweed as the current bore it relentlessly towards them.

The overburdened mother was now crying. Mrs. Plaid consoled her and dug some sweets for the children out of a capacious patent leather handbag. The man in the brown cap called loudly for a doctor, but Ned, automatically stepping forward, changed his mind and decided not to reveal himself.

What would be the point? No doctor could help that poor soul any longer. Whatever his story might have been and whatever mysterious grief or violence had terminated it, he was now nothing but a morsel for the current to digest. Best let the corpse be and preserve his own strength for tomorrow, when he might actually be able to help a living body. A nice sturdy policeman could console the public just as well as he could; probably better. No, there was no point getting involved. Today he would just be Ned, lover of architecture and music, of all structures articulate and well made, and not Dr. Abraham, patcher-up of the broken and the maimed.

Sundays were a solitary but substantial pleasure for Dr. Edward Abraham. Weekdays he barely drew breath without interruption, somebody always wanting more than he could give. So he built his own bridges, Sunday to Sunday, to carry him over the fray. The English Sabbath was a long meander along the river, following the score of whatever piece was featured at that day's concert. Whenever possible he preferred a violin solo, ideally one he might play himself. Then he could retreat into the music's shelter at odd moments after work and recover his equilibrium.

Ned's habit of walking along the river began back in Leeds when he was a boy. His father would wake him up early Sunday mornings, sometimes before the sun rose. They would dress quietly so as not to wake Mama and Alta, drink a cup of hot milky tea, stuff some thick slabs of bread and cheese in their pockets, and escape the soot-stifled Leylands ghetto just as the first merchants were setting up their wares. Zigzagging through the narrow cobbled courts and alleys, down North Street, down Vicar Lane, all the way south, Papa's acrid commentary never ceased: the banks, the churches, the shops, the railway, even the schools — all corrupt, all bought and sold. No man could be free in this society. But the river, ah, that belonged to everyone and to no one, like the air. And this *was* the River Aire, Ned always remarked, and his father always laughed.

Usually they turned east, away from the city centre, continuing until they found a likely spot under a thick-leafed tree where the ground wasn't too wet. There they ate their sandwiches and there they fished, for once equal both in expectation and in disappointment. Ned loved his father best at such moments. Chaim's loud voice and bullying melted away when the class struggle was deferred for more immediate and tangible pleasures. His parents had few enough of those. Most days they argued, spitting contempt at each other until a door slammed and his father stamped off righteously to some meeting or other about the suffering proletariat, whose problems were at once less irritating than his own and susceptible of much grander solutions.

Ned's mother barely acknowledged that his father had left the house as she turned back to her sewing machine or picked up a delicate piece of embroidery. If she heard Ned crying, she might come to his doorway and tell him not to fret. But she never came in to put comforting arms around him. He longed for those arms, unyielding as he knew they would be, but he also felt guilty, recognizing in that desire an obscure betrayal of his father. So night after night, Ned pulled the covers over his head to shut out their angry voices. Often he sang the same song over and over until he was too tired to sing any more, then let himself fall into a sad muddle of sleep.

Fishing and music had always provided the most reliable solace, and they remained linked in his imagination. Slow arts, both of them, demanding patience and attention and endless repetition. And of course silence, blessed silence, from everyone else.

Ned walked north along the river trying, ineffectually, to forget the sad body discarded on the sand back there. Strangers had gathered to peck at it. A clamour of carrion voices rose: *caw, caw, caw.* Plenty of meat for gossip; they'd be chattering about this for hours. He had thought that becoming a doctor would harden him against death, but it hadn't. And the spectacle of this anonymous soul, discarded like so much unwanted junk, touched him as his real patients, surrounded by concerned relatives, sometimes failed to. Why was that? Why should the sudden death of a complete stranger seem more significant than the slow dissolution of a sick man? Was this a particular failing in him, or was it a general rule of nature that anything unknown seemed more important than familiar things did? He didn't know and probably never would.

So he walked on, willing himself to be absorbed into the graceful scenery around him to escape the disquieting images in his mind. Slanting rays of afternoon light glanced off ships fretting at anchor, and a few low clouds, edged with red, flared into gold when the sun broke through. Ned took a deep breath and inhaled sweetness at the edge of corruption. Roses! They must still be blooming in the Temple gardens, tended by an army of custodians hiding the invisible apparatus of power under this tranquil green façade.

He came up from the Embankment at Blackfriars Bridge and nodded to the statue of Queen Victoria. She surveyed the city complacently, her broad back to the river. As formidable in effigy as she had been in life, Victoria didn't need to look at the waves to know who ruled them. But no matter how often he walked these streets, he would never truly belong to them. London tolerated his presence, as it tolerated other supplicants from other places, but its towers and law courts, its churches and banks and theatres and libraries, did not welcome him. Maybe that was why he spent so much time walking along the river — because water possessed everyone equally. Like music, it flowed around a world without borders.

Along Queen Victoria Street past the College of Arms he went, shutting his eyes against a sudden gust swirling papers along Cannon Street with a vision of the floating corpse. Had he made a mistake abandoning an old Jew, with his grey beard and lost dignity, to the unlikely mercy of an English crowd? How much, after all, do we owe our dead?

A silvery smell swam towards him: Billingsgate. But the market would be closed now, its gilded fish weathervanes shifting over the empty arcades. On the housekeeper's day off, he trolled its banks for dinner, coming home with exotica that she, priding herself on being "a good plain cook," would never touch: lobster, oysters, fish with ridiculous foreign names. He'd taught himself to cook out of necessity but continued as a diversion. Occasionally he'd even invite colleagues over, specifying exactly what wine they should bring for the elaborate meal he'd executed. Mother might or might not join his guests on such occasions, but she was never called on to be the hostess. He was well aware of how people might interpret his still living with her at thirty-two.

His mother joked that he was a better cook than she'd ever been. She had no interest at all in food, cooking and eating the absolute minimum required for health. One boiled egg and half a sliced tomato would do for lunch, a sole fillet and a handful of peas for dinner. If her meals sometimes left her family hungry, they could always fill up on bread. Mrs. Abraham never knowingly neglected her children, but she refused, on principle, to cater to them. She was impatient with confessions of hunger and fatigue or aches and pains. As far as she was concerned, people ought to be able to rise above physical discomfort. The purpose of evolution, as she saw it, was to transcend mere animal nature. So while Ned's decision to go into medicine pleased her because it would increase the family's social status, she couldn't imagine doing such a job herself. How could he bear to examine so many ugly, unwell, unwashed bodies? If *she* ever became a doctor, she declared, she would certainly have to plug her nose.

Perhaps his sense of smell was less delicate than hers. He followed it towards the market, savouring the maritime reek. Billingsgate was one of his favourite places, especially at dawn when the fishmongers unpacked crates of silver and gold and opalescent scales and built pink hills of prawns, draping them with purplish vines of octopus. Though most of the sea creatures had been killed already, they seemed so alive, just like the forest of cut flowers at Covent Garden, blazing on after their deaths.

It was strange. When people died, the life went out of them instantly. Their corpses just lay there, forlorn and reproachful, things best tidied away as quickly as possible. But the heaped bodies of fish, in their abundance and brilliant colour, gave an illusion of vitality that thrilled him and made him wish, sometimes, that he could paint. In art, at least, there is no corruption. Things stay the same forever.

Ned turned south to London Bridge, the most recent in a sequence dating back to Roman times. The original bridge had been wooden, as were various medieval structures that followed. But by the end of the twelfth century masons rebuilt the arch in stone and houses rose up upon it, making the district into a bustling neighbourhood of pin makers and booksellers. Ned would like to have seen London Bridge then, even to have lived on it, though well away from Drawbridge Tower at the south end, where the parboiled heads of traitors hung like gigantic rotting fruit. Oh, it must have been a busy place, and noisy! All day, the shriek of seagulls, the shouts of watermen, the roar of water through the arches, the clanking of mills and machinery; at night, a dazzle of moonlit waves and a forest of masts. While pedestrians tried to negotiate the narrow footpath between overhanging houses, oarsmen risked their lives guiding their boats through the churning rapids below. Above the bridge, by contrast, the Thames was placid: a lake upon which skaters danced during winter fairs. Hard to imagine this river of sludge and traffic, this tumultuous thoroughfare, suspended like that: white and still, a vast tundra in the middle of the city. Silence made solid.

Or perhaps not. Ned suddenly recalled an old riddle.

> *As I was going o'er London Bridge,*
> *I heard something crack —*
> *Not a man in England*
> *Can mend that.*

Ice, of course. There had always been, and there would always be, things no doctor could mend.

Aufschwung

Children shackled in Sunday best squirmed as the audience filled row upon row of uncomfortable folding chairs. The recital hall, normally an ominous cavern students tiptoed by with averted eyes, echoed with laughter, greetings, and nervous shrieks from those about to perform. The smell of hair tonic and perfume mingled with the resinous fragrance of an enormous Christmas tree looming at the back of the stage. From the top of the tree, a conical cardboard angel with wings of gold net surveyed the crowd with an impassive smile, as she did annually. Perhaps she thought the festivities were in her honour.

Jacob Weiss, sitting in the third row with his mother and grandfather, fixed his eyes on the angel. He remembered her from last year, when he sat in the audience thinking how much better he could play than any of the junior pianists on stage. Now he would have to prove to her — and to everyone else in the room — that he had been right. His head buzzed with furious wasps and his heart was beating too fast, but he was very happy. Music did that to him.

Good music, at any rate, not the elementary rubbish a couple of little girls were passing off as a duet to the overindulgent parents in the crowd. Their skirts were so fluffy and their legs so short, it was a wonder they could balance on the piano bench at all. They looked like a couple of fat hens on a fence! When they hopped down and tried to curtsy, their beribboned heads bobbing up and down, the resemblance was so startling that Jacob laughed out loud, annoying his mother, who whispered sternly, be polite. It would be his turn soon enough.

And it was. Somehow he was on stage, seated; somehow he had begun to play. Jacob leaned into the music as into a strong wind. He had never played a concert grand before and it seemed to him a living creature, like a beautiful black horse, responding instantly to the slightest pressure, almost playing itself. By comparison, the little upright at home was over-bright, tinny, with a stiff action that made delicacy of touch impossible. His teacher had an old, beaten-up baby grand, and until now his weekly practice on that instrument had been his greatest delight. But this new piano made possible a whole rainbow of colours.

He forgot where he was: the stuffy hall, bright lights, people coughing. The piece he had practised for months, Schumann's "Aufschwung," opened up before him, no longer a narrow alley of pollarded limes but a panorama of meadows, streams, soft green hills; here a graveyard, there a school. The wind whistled by, and he was riding the piano in the bliss of it, entirely alone. "Aufschwung" means soaring, but he never understood it like this before.

Now a steep slope, and every nerve in his body braced for the climb. At the top there was a jump. Would he find the power to get up and over? He was too small; surely the beast would throw him. No, he had made it safe to the end, and there was a collective sigh of relief from the audience. Clara, his mother, clapped involuntarily, then looked around with an apologetic smile at the other nervous parents.

Zayde glanced at his daughter-in-law. It sounded good, so why was she so worried? The boy was too serious also. He didn't play outside enough; just look how pale he was. And in that jacket he was a little man already, even seated at such a huge instrument.

The room exploded with applause. Now Zayde beamed too and stood up with the others, clapping wildly.

"Bravo!" he shouted.

Jacob bowed once, twice, then almost ran off the stage to them. "I made two mistakes, Mama. I still have trouble with the fast bit."

"Yakov, Yakov, listen how everyone's clapping. You played beautifully," said his grandfather. "Mazel tov! Don't be so hard on yourself all the time."

"Zayde's right, darling. We are so proud of you. I only wish your Aunt Alice could have been here tonight. Now sha, here comes the singer."

Jacob sat down between the two people who loved him best in the world. His heart was pounding so loudly he was surprised they couldn't hear it. But after all it was *his* heart, inside his own chest: a private music. And up there, on the stage, he hadn't thought of his mother, he hadn't thought of her even once. Because he hadn't been playing for her. Her devotion to him, her ever-present anxiety, had been drowned out by the piano.

A man Jacob had seen around the Guildhall walked quietly onto the stage. That wasn't the singer, that was Mr. Alfred Walter, an elderly piano teacher. From head to toe he was a grey man, a skeleton in an ill-fitting grey suit, with sparse grey hair combed over a pale forehead. How could someone so colourless be a match for an instrument like that? And yet he was supposed to be a distinguished musician. Obviously, you couldn't tell much about people from their appearance. Zayde was always reminding him of this, but he tended to forget.

Now a handsome man with flashing black eyes entered, carrying a violin. Unlike Mr. Walter, he wore a tuxedo. Apparently he considered himself the equal of the singer and not a mere accompanist. He bowed once from the waist and then claimed his place next to the piano as a tall, black-haired woman in a red dress took the stage. She stood at the front, looking around the room imperiously as though to command silence. Her strategy worked. The rustling and coughing subsided at once. She turned to the handsome man, nodded, and he raised his violin. Neither of them seemed to acknowledge poor Mr. Walter, who seemed more insignificant than ever next to the man in black and the woman in red.

She was a distinguished guest, a famous Hungarian mezzo-soprano, in London for two years while her husband served as cultural attaché at the embassy. She had been giving voice lessons to a few select students, and rumours of her beauty and of her elegant soirées flew freely around the chalk-smelling corridors of the school. Like the woman, the music was exotic. The violin was more than background: it was another voice, calling and responding, now plaintive, now fierce. The singer and the violinist rarely glanced at each other, though they seemed to be having a private conversation against the unobtrusive harmonies of Mr. Walter's piano. They were like a rose and a briar, entwined against the grey wall that supported them and set them off. Some of the older members of the audience consulted their programmes again to cover up growing agitation, even embarrassment: "Il Tramonto," by

Ottorino Respighi. This was not what they had expected at a Christmas concert — these dark strangers with their haunting music. And besides, it was going on much too long.

Clara was surprised to find tears in her eyes. She thought she had wept herself out while Jacob played, but the violin always moved her, and this piece, with its sad urgency, called to parts of her she preferred not to remember. Maybe the old people around her shuffled their programmes for the same reason she was hugging Jacob so tightly. Soon he too would be aroused by such passions, but for now music was just a charming puzzle, a game of virtuosity. Still, he had that absolute focus, that listening which hinted at unusual depth of feeling, and she worried for him.

The musicians fell silent and bowed their heads. The audience was quiet for a moment before scattered applause built to a resounding acknowledgement. The singer waited a beat, then lifted her head and gestured to the instrumentalists. As they rose to their feet and joined her at the front of the stage, Clara observed that the violinist was shorter than the woman by a head, though equally dark and good-looking, with straight brows and unusually dark, deep-set eyes. The programme identified him as Dr. Edward Abraham. A doctor of music perhaps? At any rate, it was a pompous title to flaunt at a children's recital. Though Clara had enjoyed the music, she thought she would probably dislike the man.

Pushing back chairs, gathering their coats and bags, the audience released the musicians into a field of random noise. The world resumed its familiar ragged contours; attention flickered here and there, sparrows gathering seed in the snow. Colours, sounds, smells — everything became diffuse and,

at the same time, intrusive. Bodies that had been weight-
less suddenly sagged under the insistence of gravity: shoes
pinched, hats itched, bellies rumbled. Released from their
spell, the audience filed out of the recital hall to a long table
covered in white damask holding silver urns of tea and coffee. Pretty biscuits, coconut-sprinkled or chocolate-dipped,
cherry- or almond-centred, swirled on doily-covered plat-
ters. Jacob ran ahead, cramming one chocolate biscuit in his
mouth and two into his pocket to take home for his sister
Evelyn and brother Daniel.

"Good work, Weiss," said an older boy, who had opened
the show with a competent if unimaginative rendition of the
Trumpet Voluntary.

"Thanks," mumbled Jacob, chewing. "You too."

Clara came up behind her son and congratulated the other
boy, who stared slack-jawed at Zayde, trailing behind in a
long black coat and a black hat, then clutched his trumpet
case across his chest like a shield. The bent old man, noticing
the trumpeter's discomfort and not wanting to cause a problem for Jacob, said he'd like to sit by himself for a while and
found a quiet corner from which to observe the gathering.
A habitué of the East End ghetto, he rarely found himself in
this kind of crowd: English, wealthy, blond, and glittering. It
was a novelty but at the same time somewhat overwhelming.
Even frightening, though he'd never admit it.

Clara was about to join her father-in-law when the trumpeter's parents stepped forward and introduced themselves
as the Prescotts. Mrs. Prescott fussed a bit with her son's tie
to emphasize the prestige of the school it advertised, a man-
oeuvre wasted on Jacob and Clara, who failed to recognise
it.

"What did you think of that Hungarian woman?" she

asked, after informing them that her name was Maude. She was pretty in the Victorian fashion of her name, dressed all in palest pink, with pale skin and paler hair.

"I thought she sang beautifully. To be honest, I never expected to hear someone so professional at this concert."

"But what kind of an example was that for the children?"

"What do you mean?" Clara asked, starting to feel uncomfortable and hoping no one else could overhear their conversation.

"Well, my dear, it was decadent, foreign and decadent, don't you think? The way that violinist stared at her, as though we couldn't see him. After all, she's married, you know, to the Hungarian ambassador or someone like that." Her colourless lashes gave her eyes a rabbity look as they darted around the room, and her little upturned nose seemed to quiver with indignation.

"Oh look, Jacob, there's Miss Westerham. Shall we go say hello? Excuse me please, it was a pleasure to meet you," said Clara, steering Jacob, who was preoccupied with a glass of lemonade, in the direction of his madly waving piano teacher.

"Hello, hello there, Jacob. I've been looking for you! That was excellent, really excellent," Miss Westerham bellowed, fluffing up his hair. Clara had wetted it down for the concert, but it needed little encouragement from Miss Westerham to spring back into unruly brown waves.

Jacob didn't mind. He adored his teacher, and a word of real praise from her meant more than any number of compliments from his indulgent family. To them, everything he did was beautiful, brilliant, amazing, extraordinary. But Miss Westerham always caught him whenever he faked it, playing too quickly, in order to get through a difficult part, or too loudly, out of impatience or inattention.

"No flying thumbs?" he grinned up at her. "No ski slopes?"

"Not that I could see from where I sat! No, really Jacob, you did very well for someone giving his first big public performance. Not everyone can relax in front of a crowd. You have to be able to concentrate on the music and forget where you are."

"Actually," she continued, "I was just talking about you with Dr. Abraham. You know, the violinist? Who played with the opera singer? He was very impressed with your Schumann, so I suggested that you try to work on something together for the next Guildhall recital in early May. It would be so good for you to start playing with other people, Jacob. What do you think?"

"He's a doctor?"

"Yes. Why do you ask?"

"Because he plays the violin."

"So? Who says you can only do one thing with your life?"

"I don't know. I never really thought about it. I've never met a doctor who played the violin before, that's all," Jacob said, starting to feel a little foolish.

Everyone was always asking him if he was going to be a famous musician when he grew up. No one had ever suggested that you could play music well and still do other things. Papa had been a shopkeeper like Zayde; Uncle Sidney was a furrier and so was his son Bernard; cousin Paul made eyeglasses. None of them played music at all, they just seemed to work all the time. Well, Paul liked to play chess, but that didn't really count. Anyhow, Jacob could already beat him.

"Jacob, you're woolgathering."

"Sorry, Miss Westerham," he replied automatically. He was used to being reprimanded for not paying attention.

"Well, never mind. Here they come, so you can discuss the plan in person."

And indeed, sweeping towards them was the beautiful Hungarian lady. Her gold earrings swung and sparkled as she inclined her head this way and that, acknowledging the murmured compliments of those she passed. A half-smile played upon her lips, which were painted the same red as her dress. Jacob thought he had never seen anyone so wonderful. Clara smoothed her wrinkled skirt over her hips and wished she'd at least had her hair done for the occasion.

"Ah, the little prodigy," the singer exclaimed, giving Jacob a big smile and extending a hand, which the boy shook with some timidity. Even her nails were scarlet! "And you must be his proud mother."

"Madame Tabori, I'm so honoured to meet you. I enjoyed your singing very much."

"Thank you. It has been a charming affair. And you must call me Magda, please. Ah, finally! Here is Dr. Abraham, who has a proposal for your talented son."

Ned, who had been hanging back uncomfortably, stepped forward. How had he allowed himself to be cornered this way? The last thing he needed to add to his busy life was a temperamental little pianist. Not that Jacob wasn't good, he was very good, but surely the boy would refuse to practice or burst into tears every time he made a mistake. He was just so young.

"How do you do?" he said, shaking hands first with the mother, who was red-haired and rather pretty, though un-fashionably dressed in a navy blue skirt and cardigan, and then the son, who had a smear of chocolate on his cheek and looked even smaller than he had on stage.

Ned felt his heart sink. The piano teacher had emphasized what a kindness it would be for him to spend some time with this fatherless boy, so how could he refuse without seeming hard-hearted? And why was Magda smiling at him in that maddening way? She knew how much he hated being manipulated.

"Tell them your idea, Edward dear," she said, still smiling.

"Well, yes . . . but actually, this isn't *my* idea. Miss Westerham came up with it, and I'm not sure it's really practical," he began. He tried to keep his voice pleasant, but he couldn't disguise his lack of enthusiasm.

The mother noticed it right away. Her hands went to her son's narrow shoulders, and she pulled the boy towards her almost roughly.

"Oh, I'm sure you're right, Dr. Abraham. Jacob isn't ready for this yet, he's much too young."

"Nonsense!" cried Miss Westerham, so loudly that the crowd milling around them turned to see what was going on.

Ned became even more embarrassed; there was nothing he disliked more than the scrutiny of strangers. But the stout, dowdy piano teacher was oblivious, as usual. She wore bright colours because she liked them, she spoke *fortissimo* when she was excited, and she tried to persuade people to do what she thought they ought to do. It never occurred to her to be tentative or apologetic. Why should she? She always seemed to know exactly what she wanted.

What must it be like not to care what others thought of you? Something altogether outside Ned's experience, perhaps reserved only for those whose history and geography flowed imperturbably along the same well-worn channels. He had heard Miss Westerham say that her family had inhabited the county of Kent for so long that they still remembered the evil day in 1066 when William the Conqueror gave their land to Bishop Odo of Bayeux. Sometimes she joked that this humiliation accounted for her atrocious French, since resistance to the Norman invasion was innate in the Westerham family. She even claimed to be allergic to French music and French cuisine, French literature and especially French perfume.

"Not only is Jacob old enough, but he needs the challenge of ensemble work. Violinists always play with other people, don't they, Dr. Abraham, but pianists can get so isolated. It's not healthy for them or for the music. Just because pianists can make their own harmony doesn't mean that they ought to be alone all the time."

"Well," said Ned, smiling for the first time, "sometimes violinists need to be alone too. I certainly do. And there's some wonderful solo repertoire. But I agree that having a balance is what's important. Balance in all things, right, Jacob? Like the ancient Greeks, you know."

"Yes, sir," said Jacob, who had no idea what the man was talking about or why the grownups were getting so tense. His mother was angry, he could feel it in her hands, clutching his shoulders. When he turned around to look at her, she had that don't-say-another-word-or-I'll-shout mask on. He kept looking for somewhere to put down his empty glass. Wasn't it time to go home yet?

"Then it's settled," Miss Westerham declared. "I was thinking of the early Mozart sonatas because they're so easy. It would be good for Jacob to start off with something where the only challenge is for him to work with another musician. But let me know if you two prefer something else."

"Miss Westerham, please don't put the doctor on the spot like this. I'm sure he's far too busy to accommodate a child. And besides, Jacob has a great deal of schoolwork these days. I really don't think it's a good idea," said Clara, getting more and more flustered.

Zayde, who had been sitting quietly in his corner with a cup of tea, was now working his way toward them with their coats on his arm. She must not let her father-in-law get involved in this fiasco. He would bristle at the superior attitude of the doctor and the languid confidence of Madame Tabori and, in his desire to protect Jacob, would inevitably make one of his rabbinical speeches and embarrass them all. But nothing must spoil Jacob's triumph today.

Ned gave her a direct look for the first time and noted her raised chin and flushed cheeks. The heightened colour made her green eyes shine fiercely. It was clear that this woman was no fool. She was proud, and proud of her son, and determined to keep him from being hurt. Ned found himself obscurely moved by the tenderness with which her lips brushed Jacob's hair. Suddenly he resolved to go through with the thing. The Mozart sonatas Miss Westerham had suggested were essentially keyboard pieces; it would be a chance for the boy to shine. His violin would have little to do but provide support. How terrible could it be, after all?

"Oh, it's all right, Mrs. Weiss. If Jacob's game, so am I. What do you say, young man? Would you like to try some Mozart?"

"I guess so," said Jacob, not sure what response was expected of him anymore.

Luckily, his grandfather arrived at that moment and asked

if they were ready to go home. Clara felt compelled to introduce Zayde to Ned and Magda, but to her surprise the singer, far from laughing at the quaint old man, gracefully produced a couple of halting phrases in Yiddish. He, in turn, became a model of gallantry. It turned out that his late wife had been a connoisseur of opera in general and of sopranos in particular, a fact that Clara had never suspected. Compliments flew all around, and the party broke up merrily after all.

"You should have seen your face, darling, it was too funny," said Magda, plucking Ned's cigarette from his mouth to light her own.

Uncorseted, her figure was smaller and softer that it appeared on stage. In a loose, flowery kimono, with dark hair tumbling to her shoulders, she appeared almost girlish. The effect was assisted by the rosy candlelight she insisted on for their trysts. Ned recognized the calculation and appreciated it. There was no subterfuge involved, after all; a taste for beauty was what had brought them together in the first place. A taste for beauty and a certain self-possession others mistook for indifference.

They had much in common, he thought. In pursuit of their goals, they had simplified their lives. Although Magda had married, she was childless. She seemed to spend most of her time reading, visiting her dressmaker, going to galleries, eating in restaurants, and making music. A life Ned's father would have condemned as socially irresponsible, even parasitic, but one Ned might well have preferred to the compliant balance of duty and pleasure he had negotiated for himself.

He was not in love with Magda. Indeed, Magda teased

him that what he liked best about her *was* that he was not in love with her. That and the fact that she had a convenient understanding with a husband she had no intention of leaving. Ned had a long history of affairs with married women. He found them restful; they lacked the expectation that he would change his life for them. And they did not have that unnerving vivacity, that predatory smiling he associated with his sister's friends in Manchester. On the other hand, there was a sadness to these married women, a tincture of melancholy, that he recognized the moment it seeped out. But it had nothing to do with him. If it threatened to flood the relationship, he simply moved on. Something else he'd learned from his father.

He wasn't ready to move on from Magda, however; she was beautiful and talented and witty, and very gratifying in bed. Best of all, she loved to talk seriously about music, a pleasure he had foregone since his student days in Leeds when he had played in the symphony before determining on a career in medicine instead. Most people assumed Ned gave up music for practical reasons, for money or reputation. Only Magda and his sister Alta understood that he'd really capitulated to doubt. Deep in his heart, Edward Abraham né Abramowicz knew he'd never be a virtuoso. He'd be good, but never good enough.

Ned found it humiliating to do things poorly and intolerable to do them no more than adequately. A life as one of many second violins in a provincial orchestra would surely have been a life of disappointment. Besides, he hated being in a group: the endless chatter, the mutual obligation. He hated having to play the assigned repertoire. And too many nights trying to sleep while his father held noisy meetings in their flat had convinced him never to join a collective. On the other hand, the rhetoric of those meetings had persuaded him that no free man should have to endure a boss. He was never quite sure how he had found himself confiding these things to Magda Tabori, of all people. Somehow, she always managed to elicit his secrets without imparting any of her own. It seemed as though she required something from him in exchange for her favours, some little token to symbolize that he was not her master even if she was his mistress. For the same reason, she often laughed at him: he was younger, after all, and not as worldly as he thought.

Usually he didn't mind. But tonight there was a challenge in her tone, neither professional nor sexual. It had to do with something she saw in his character, something she had appraised and found lacking. He didn't like this kind of intimacy. It had no place in their relationship.

"Why do you keep teasing me?" he asked. "I don't understand why you had to join forces with that bloody cow Westerham. You always say you can't bear those old maids in their musical convent. Did you really think that boy was so amazing? It seems to me that eleven-year-old prodigies lurk around every corner these days."

She laughed again. "I certainly was not joining forces, as you so dramatically put it, although I must say that La Belle Westerham's turquoise frock set off my red one quite nicely. No, I found the idea delightful, that's all. That boy, Jacob: he really reminded me of you, Edward, of how I imagine you as a child. So I thought it would be fun to see you play together, big and little at the same time."

"I was nothing like that," said Ned. "He had chocolate all over his face, for God's sake."

"Don't be ridiculous. You know that's not what I'm talking about."

36

"You mean he's a Yid."

"I mean he is beautiful."

"A beautiful little Yid."

"Well, what's wrong with that? Are you so ashamed of your family?"

"Aren't you?" he countered.

"First of all, I'm only half-Jewish and Stefan is Catholic, so my situation is quite different. And secondly, I am not ashamed, it simply is not relevant."

"If it's not relevant, why didn't you go to Germany with Stefan?"

"I love singing in Germany. My God, I had my greatest triumph at Bayreuth, as Venus in *Tannhauser*. But I will not go there while a bunch of bureaucrats at the Reich Chamber of Culture decide who should or should not be allowed to make music. They are all lunatics, and that Hitler's the worst."

"Lunatic or not, he's getting stronger every day," Ned remarked. "Since the Austrian putsch last summer, the Nazis are more popular than ever."

"But I'm sure most Germans are against him, really. They are just using him, you know, as a kind of protest to the world. That is what Stefan says, anyhow. He says the real power is the industrialists who are getting rich from rearmament."

"He's awfully naïve for a diplomat, your Stefan. Anyway, why should I trust his judgement when he's foolish enough to abandon a beautiful woman like you?"

"When it comes to politics, even I trust him." Magda laughed. "And he has not abandoned me, as you very well know. I make my own decisions."

"Well, then, allow me to make mine. And don't try to influence me when it comes to who I make music with."

"But I thought you agreed to play with the boy?"

"I did, but I regret it already."

"But why? It is wonderful to find such musicality in someone so young. Not that it has anything to do with age, because music takes you right out of your body. Or no, not out of it, but into the deepest part of it, so that you are not a child, not a man or a woman, but something singing. A song."

"That's very pretty, Magda. Is that what you tell all the young men who admire your décolletage? That you are not a woman, just a song?"

At this, she put down her brandy snifter, uncurled from the armchair, and crossed to where he sat sullenly hunched in front of the fireplace. Magda slowly unknotted the belt of her kimono, her angry eyes never leaving his face. She let the brightly patterned cloth slip to the floor and stood naked before the dancing flames, challenging him.

Instantly, he regretted his petulance. He wanted her. He stood up, smiling, and reached out. But she pushed him away, her palms flat against his chest, her face blank.

"Go home, Edward. I do not permit anyone to speak to me like that."

"Then let's not speak at all," he murmured, grabbing her hand and kissing it, a parody of submission. But Magda was too wise for him, and her voice was very cold.

"You forget that you need me more than I need you," she said.

"I don't need anyone!"

"Everyone needs someone, my darling. Even you. On the day you admit that to yourself, you will find the possibility of happiness."

"Oh bloody hell, Magda, don't patronize me. I'm sorry if

I was rude, but you have to admit that you were provoking me."

"How, Edward? By trying to talk seriously for once?"

"That's not fair, and you know it. We talk seriously all the time. And *you're* the one who never wants to give anything away. But I tell you everything. For God's sake, you know more about me than anyone except my sister."

"I am very sorry to hear it."

"There you go again. What's the matter with you to-night?"

"I don't know, really. I think it was that little boy. He was . . . so pure. And there was his mother, and his grandfather, the three of them so nervous together, so proud. Like peasants at the palace, you know? I often see such people when I go to official things with Stefan, hanging back a little, shabby, awkward, but their eyes shining like the moon."

"The Weiss family are hardly peasants, Magda, just ordinary Londoners. Don't you think you're romanticizing a bit?"

"Perhaps, but still I have this ache inside. What will happen to children like Jacob when they grow older and things don't come easily anymore? Hard work will not be enough. We all need so much luck."

"Well, *you've* certainly been lucky."

To his surprise, she didn't answer right away, but slowly picked up the discarded kimono and put it back on. Finally she replied, her voice pensive but her face turned away from him so he couldn't guess what she was thinking.

"Lucky? In some ways. My voice is still good. And Stefan lets me do what I want."

"And what about me?"

"You, my beautiful little Yid, should go. I am tired."

She handed him his jacket and tie, which he had flung onto a chair. Her back was to the fire now, and she was all silhouette, flaring into gold at the edges, into golden sparks and whorls and plumes around the darker mass of her hair — darker still at the centre, unknown after all. An image he carried with him into the rainy night, under the steaming lamps of London, over the bridges, home.

Jewish Music

Danny's round belly glistened with soap, iridescent bubbles sliding and popping under the scrubbing flannel. He was a frothy fat beast, Clara declared, and Evvie giggled, holding her slippery little brother tighter. Clara's red hair frizzed up in the steam, unmanageable, but luckily none of her children had inherited her mop. All had nice thick brown hair that shone beautifully after a wash. The hard part was getting it clean; the baby screamed and flailed and got shampoo in his eyes, and Evvie, co-operative enough when being lathered, flinched at the rinse. The water could never be hot enough for her, skinny thing. She always left the bath shivering and ran at once to the fire to steam herself dry.

But Clara loved the bath. Oh, how she loved it! These firm little bodies, melon-smooth, skin tight over quick-pumping hearts, the delicate tracery of ribs. They were seals, they were otters, hers and not hers, not entirely human yet. Sometimes, on dull afternoons, she got in the bath with the little ones and they played fishing or mermaids or pirates. Squealing, they slid down her belly. One moment, her body was just soft furniture, their playground, and the next, pure solace. As they were for her.

It was a terrible waste of hot water. Leonard would have complained, but she didn't care. It was lovely, all that quick clean flesh caressing her tired body, the kisses. When Danny had been a new baby and things were so awful, sometimes she even nursed him in the bath, both of them half-asleep in the heat. Lying there with eyes closed, her womb contracting rhythmically in time to his suckling, it was as if the cord between them had never been severed. She was scoured by waves inside and out; she was a sea-thing, beyond the pain and bewilderment of dying husband and sad children. Deep in her core something extraordinary throbbed. Not happiness, nothing so brilliant and transitory, but contentment.

But how could that be, with Leonard getting weaker every day and Zayde lumbering around, bereft? With Jacob getting into fights at school, and Evvie, still frail herself from croup, toddling in to demand, "Papa, up!"? How could that be when Clara lay in the bath with tears running down her face, unable to think beyond the next day's meals and medicines, the endless washing of stinking sheets and stinking nappies, to the years ahead alone with three children? She was only twenty-seven; no one had warned her this could happen. Where were her parents when she needed them most? She was already an orphan. Now she would be a widow as well.

These days there was only — and always — Alice. Alice bustling in with a pot of soup or a basket of new cherries, library books or a paintbox for the children. Alice opening windows and fluffing up pillows, shooing her away for a nap or a walk in the park with little Evvie to put colour in their cheeks. When they were younger, her sister had been a selfish person: resentful, envious, always complaining that she'd been hard done by. But since her own children had grown up, she'd reached a plateau of satisfaction and could care for others. Even if much of what she offered was somehow crude, a parody of competence and sympathy, it was sincere. And Alice's prattle was easier to bear than Zayde's desolate silence, a silence full of unanswerable questions.

Clara herself couldn't focus on anything but whatever task was most pressing at the moment. She lived a succession of crises between brief dreamless naps, flinging herself into sleep like a soldier on the front lines, and waking at the least whimper from the frail man on the bed or the plump infant in the cradle. The cot she slept in felt luxuriously large since the space was hers and hers alone. Sleep was normally the only time she *was* alone and could withdraw her awareness from others. It was a normal part of having a new baby, the fine attunement of her senses to his. And not just him, of course, the other children too. They were so imperious, so utterly present, even as Leonard became less and less distinct each day. Had she shut him out in her rage at his dying? Or was he quietly, courteously, taking himself away, so as not to be a bother? Whichever it was, he had conspired to help her put the children first. Everything must continue, baths and stories and meals; she must keep steady so they would not be unmoored by grief and chaos and so she would not drift away from them entirely into terror.

She still kept the children close, as much to protect herself as them. Too close, perhaps, Alice would say. Did say. Two years after Leonard's death they continued to cling to her, and she knew she encouraged it. Most nights, one or the other little one ended up in her bed, curled into her warmth even as she warmed herself on their round sweet shoulders, round sweet heads, the biscuity smell that came from their skin even while they slept. She held them tight, tight, never to let go.

"Mama, come in, come in with us, Mama," Evvie crooned.

It was easy for Clara to say no, with Jacob downstairs practising the piano. She worried he might feel left out. Too old for naked play, he was still young enough to miss it and to need a special hug from time to time in compensation. But any day that too would be taken from him. And also from her: she could feel it coming, a cold draft in the space between them. Her head acknowledged that this was inevitable, though her pulse drummed *too soon*.

"No, my darlings, we must get you off to bed. Danny-boy, let me see your piggies. Are they all clean?"

And a smooth little foot poked through the bubbles, the boy himself almost going under in the process. Evvie grabbed him, responsible as ever.

What was Jacob playing? She'd been humming along absent-mindedly but now found herself adding words.

> *It's time to dry your little toes,*
> *It's time to blow your little nose.*
> *We cannot linger on each finger,*
> *We cannot stay in here to play,*
> *Tomorrow is another day.*

"You always say that, Mama. There are so many tomorrows, aren't there? Every day is a tomorrow," said Evvie, who at four was soberly preoccupied with time, with getting it right.

"Yes, my clever girl. What do you call the day that comes before this?"

"Yesterday."

"And this day, the day we're in, is called what?"

"Today!" triumphantly from Evvie, and "Today!" a happy echo from her brother.

"That's right. Before we get to a day it's *tomorrow*, while we're in it, it's *today*, and when it's finished, it's *yesterday*."

"So every day has three names, Mama, just like me! Evelyn Rebecca Weiss," said Evvie, highly satisfied that the rules of the universe conformed to those of her own identity.

"Well, that's a thought, isn't it?" said Clara, mopping ineffectually at a puddle on the floor. She should just leave the cleanup for later and get these two to sleep.

Had Jacob finished his lessons? She usually asked, although she needn't bother. He was such a conscientious student, even when he found the work boring, whereas she'd always had a hard time doing anything she didn't enjoy. He must have inherited his good work habits from his father, whom she missed every time she struggled to balance her household accounts.

Leonard had tried so hard to take good care of her, but in some ways he'd made things too easy. After he'd gone, she really had no understanding of money at all. Thank God for Alice and Sidney, getting her through that first year. Of course, she'd been lucky that Leonard hadn't believed in living on credit and they'd paid off the house right away. She'd been even luckier that Papa's investments had survived the Depression. And things were getting easier now, especially with the children — look how nicely they played together. And here's Evvie, her hair brushed, and into her nightgown all by herself!

Ned loves his violin. That is to say, there is nothing else in his life about which he feels the same constantly fluctuating yet compelling mixture of familiarity and wonder, admiration and resentment — those waves of passion which, if they passed between two individuals, we would describe as love. And yet it boasts no aristocratic Cremona ancestry. It's just an ordinary fiddle, manufactured by Hills of London, purveyors of fine stringed instruments.

But maybe that's a good thing; maybe that's why the wood sings so richly. Its gorgeous sienna tones are tuned to the grey vibrations of Albion. No nostalgia for the distant Mediterranean haunts Ned's violin. It is at home here, as he is, or as much at home as either of them can be anywhere, with the deeper conviction inside them that no earthly home is ever enough.

And this current that sings between them, where does it originate? In the uptake of glucose in Ned's brain that fires neurons in his motor cortex, then leapfrogs from synapse to synapse down his spinal cord, contracting some muscles in his arm and relaxing others, the resulting torque in his elbow moving the bow back and forth fluently across the strings? Or in the strings themselves, their variant length and thickness resisting the sticky resinous pull of the bow, transferring protesting tremors across the bridge to the sound-post and deep inside the resonating body of the instrument?

The violin sounds like a voice. Its belly is made of spruce, soft and yielding, its back of hard maple, and music is amplified between the two just like the voice inside a singer's chest, from pliable belly to rigid back, the same. Even its shape is human, womanly. But what is its song made of? Horsehair and resin and wood and varnish and metal. On the other hand, of what is the human voice made but folds of tissue, oscillating muscle, and a puff of air? A humble apparatus but democratic. If the fiddle is the poor man's instrument, the voice belongs even to a beggar.

Sometimes Ned classifies his patients' voices according to the poetic typology of Henricus Cornelius Agrippa, whose four-hundred-year-old treatise, *De occulta philosophia*, relates the four voice parts to cosmic elements. The bass singer represents the earth; the tenor, water; the alto, air; the soprano, fire. Sometimes he takes the analogy further, likening their diseases to the musical modes Agrippa identified with phlegm and bile and blood, a veritable opera of pathology. And sometimes he forgets his patients' names, staring right through them into their wheezing lungs and palsied limbs. He too is an instrument maker, or at least a restorer of faulty resonators, cracked bows, and broken reeds.

"How long have you felt like this, Mrs. Guttman?" Ned asked the old lady in rusty black. She looked up at him with frightened eyes, eyes of luminous unflecked blue: a small child peering out of a deeply wrinkled face, as from behind her mother's skirts.

"Yesterday after dinner it started. The pain . . . I thought maybe I ate something bad. But then it went on all night, so this morning I called my daughter. She wanted to take me to the hospital, but I said if I go in, I don't come out, like my poor Yussel, alav ha-sholom." She started to cry, then gasped and put her hand to her chest again.

Ned, who didn't like her pallor, the sheen of perspiration on her face, or the trembling in her hands, turned to the daughter. Surreptitiously, he glanced at the chart Miss Salmon had given him: Judith Schwartz, an observant woman, six children, he'd delivered the last two. Another would be coming soon by the looks of her. Then she could expect a prolapsed uterus, if things took their usual course. Female troubles, they said, as though the men had nothing to do with it, off studying the Talmud all day.

He spoke very clearly; she was in a trance of anxiety, alternately touching her mother's shoulder and wringing her own chapped hands. She wore only a gold wedding band, no watch, no jewellery, although her grey crepe dress was fashionable enough, with its white collar and cuffs and discreet pattern of white polka dots. A matching tam covered her hair, which, judging by her eyebrows, was probably black. Occasionally, out of habit, she tucked an imaginary strand back under the crown.

"Mrs. Schwartz, I could examine your mother here, but I think we'd be better off sending her over to the hospital for more extensive tests. I'll call for an ambulance, and you can accompany her to the casualty ward."

"Can't you come with us, Dr. Abraham? Please, I told her you would take care of us yourself. She's so afraid."

"You'll be in excellent hands, believe me, and your mother will be much safer there."

"Safer? How?"

"Well, for example, they might decide to keep her overnight for observation. Does she live alone?"

Now the younger woman began to cry. This was apparently a sensitive issue.

"Yes, yes. After my father — may he rest in peace — died last year, she stayed with us for a couple of months, but she always kept going back to her flat to check on things, and finally, you know, she insisted that it was time to go home. She's a stubborn woman, doctor, and she wanted to be in her own place."

"I'm sure that was the best situation for her," Ned said gently. "These things are always difficult. Now, I'm going to call the hospital, and then my nurse, Miss Salmon, will help you when the ambulance comes. Just relax. Everything will be fine."

The words, said by rote, nonetheless conveyed warm conviction. Ned was justly proud of his bedside manner. He was not one of those physicians who believed telling the truth was always the best course of action. On the contrary, dissimulation was a necessary tool of his medical practice; unless death was imminent, he preferred to let everyone be hopeful. After all, hope itself was a very potent medicine, and it looked like Mrs. Guttman needed a stiff dose.

There was a commotion down the hall, and then Miss Salmon glided into the room. Not one blond hair was out of place and her uniform was spotless. If anyone could convince his patients that Ned had things under control, it was this paragon of efficiency. With the old lady tottering between them, she and poor Mrs. Schwartz managed to get to the waiting room, where two uniformed attendants relieved them of their unresisting charge. All the other patients crowded to the window to watch their progress out to the waiting vehicle. There was a fair bit of speculation, nodding, and tongue clucking before people settled back into their private meditations. Ned, who had observed the scene from the nurse's office, nipped across the hall to get a quick cup of tea before the next patient. Earl Grey. No sugar.

He had chosen this surgery especially for its convenient

location a few blocks from Hackney Hospital. Originally a flat like the one above, in which he lived with his mother, it had been fitted out as a modern office. Patients waited in what had been the sitting room, reading magazines under a pleasant row of botanical prints. The former dining room was now the nurse's station, the kitchen and scullery the dispensary; one bedroom served for examination and another as his private study. This last retained a memory of bourgeois life, with oak panelling, well-stocked bookshelves, and even a surprisingly gaudy glass chandelier. There was a faded oriental carpet on the floor and a green banker's lamp on the paper-strewn desk. By contrast, the other rooms had been stripped and painted a hygienic white and their oak floors insulated with grey linoleum across which Miss Salmon's rubber-soled shoes strode soundlessly.

Dr. Abraham's office was the domain of someone acutely conscious of first impressions. A visitor would encounter no dust on the philodendron, no litter in the wastebaskets, no disturbing smells in the spotlessly clean lavatory. Conversely, a welcoming clutter waited in his study. A faint odour of tobacco hung upon the air and accumulated in the heavy damask drapes, and instead of floral prints, some old and modestly valuable music manuscripts graced the wall. Generally, Ned preferred not to see patients there but did all his business with them in the bright impersonal light of the examination room.

He would check up on Mrs. Guttman at the end of the day, feeling confident that she would last that long. He was not optimistic about her long-term recovery, however. Lonely old people with heart disease were not good candidates for rehabilitation. Waiting for his immediate attention were a workman with a twisted ankle, a child who refused to eat, a coughing tailor, and a woman with a bad burn needing her dressings changed. Only the tailor really worried him. A veteran of the East End sweatshops, a lifetime of inhaled lint clogged his lungs; tuberculosis was always a possibility in such cases. The white plague, they called it.

For fifty years now, every greenhorn just off the boat ended up squeezed into the squalid workshop of someone who'd been there just a little longer. A dozen or twenty souls would be crammed into a flat meant for a single family. Windows were shut tight against blowing soot; the air was choked with fibres from the wool the pressers continually damped down before ironing; babies cried, dinner was cooked, schoolwork was done, the sick were tended, all in the same tiny space. Tailors didn't even stop work to eat; they chewed bread and drank tea, hunched over endlessly whirring machines.

A year or two later, the situation would be reversed; the master would have lost everything and be slaving for his former employee. By their outward demeanour, however, no one could have told the two apart. Both were thin, pale, shabby, and desperate; both coughed deeply and habitually.

Growing up, Ned had never been allowed to forget the indignities heaped upon the bowed shoulders of such people. Even when there were no meetings at home or his father was in a jovial mood, singing rather than lecturing, a framed portrait of Bakunin glared down at him from the mantelpiece. When he was little, he thought Bakunin was God; when he got older, he pretended he was Grandpa; older still, he realized either characterization would do. His parents possessed no family pictures. They didn't even have birth certificates.

"Were you listening to my practice, Mum? Did you recognize that piece?" Jacob asked, dipping toast into a mug of warm milk. Music always made him hungry.

Clara was skimming the fat from a pot of chicken soup. She liked to cook at night, cook and read, to get a head start on the morning. She'd long ago resolved not to be the kind of mother who spent all day cleaning house, sad and bothered, shooing her children out of the way. Instead she played with them. They ventured out on long walks of discovery and might come home with anything: the ragged halo of a bird's nest, a fragment of eggshell lodged in it like a letter from departed tenants; chestnuts to roast on the fire, almost as sweet as their perfume; watercress icy cold from the stream; gaily striped snail shells like holiday umbrellas.

At the same time, it was a relief when the little ones were tucked safely away and she could chat with Jacob in the kitchen, and a relief yet again when he went upstairs to read in bed and she was finally alone. Her body dissolving. No one's mother.

"To be honest, I couldn't hear very well, Danny was splashing so much. But if I had to guess, I'd say . . . Mendelssohn?"

She'd been a decent pianist herself and still liked to play sometimes for pleasure. But she'd never had Jacob's extraordinary talent and remained a little amazed by it, as though she'd planted some reliable English perennial, a delphinium or rose, and a bird of paradise had bloomed in her garden instead. Amazed and sometimes, if she were totally honest, jealous.

"Good guess! It *is* Mendelssohn, one of the *Songs without Words*, he wrote scads of them. Mostly they don't have names either, just numbers, though people sometimes give them made-up names. I think that's silly, don't you? To give a piece of music a nickname?"

"Oh, I don't know, my love. A nickname can be affectionate, like when I call you Jakey or you call me Mum. So with music, maybe a nickname just means that people like it. Maybe it reminds them of something important, a place or a person, and the title the composer gave it doesn't seem to fit very well with the feelings they have for it."

"Well, maybe. I like the idea of 'Bee's Wedding,' even though I know it's not really what Mendelssohn called it. And it helps me get the right feeling, I can see that. But Miss Westerham said the whole idea of them being songs without words was that people should just listen to the music for itself, without making things up. Aren't we supposed to do what the composer wanted?"

"Probably most people find that hard. I know I do. Even if it's just colours, the movement of colours, or a happy or sad feeling, music usually makes me think of something."

She turned the flame down low under the soup kettle, wiped her hands on a towel, and sat down with her son, her oldest, her philosopher. It always gave her such joy to talk to him like this.

"You know, when I was little, I liked to sit with my eyes closed and imagine a whole ballet when I listened to music, costumes and all. I could never remember any of it afterwards, but while the music played the illusion was as real as if I weren't making it up. Everything was just *there*."

She sighed inwardly. It had been a long time since she'd been swept away like that, by music or anything else.

"Mum, did you know that Mendelssohn was Jewish?" Jacob asked. He had a habit of changing subjects suddenly, following the stream of his own thoughts.

"Well, his people converted, didn't they?"

"His father did, so he could get some land or something. It's kind of strange though, because the grandfather was a really important philosopher, so you wouldn't expect them to abandon their religion like that. Zayde wanted me to play some Jewish music for him, so I asked Miss Westerham for some, but there's not very much unless you count people like Mendelssohn."

"I know."

"But why is that?"

"Oh, Jacob, it's so complicated." This time she sighed outright. "The main problem, I think, is that in the old days, we weren't allowed to go to regular schools, or enter professions like law or medicine, or work for the government. Most Jews were poor and isolated, living in tiny villages with no access to concerts or art galleries. And to be honest, I think people felt that if they allowed their children to learn too much about the outside world, they might lose them. So it was their fault too, for shutting everything out. Even your grandfather was never really educated except to read Hebrew and discuss the Torah. That was all his parents could give him, and then, by thirteen, he had to go to work."

"But he's the smartest person I know," Jacob cried. "And he speaks so many languages — English, Yiddish, Polish, Russian, Hebrew . . . maybe more."

"Well, of course, not all education comes from school. But someone like him would never have ended up as a peddler if he weren't born Jewish. He might have gone to university and been a great scholar. He might have been Doctor Weiss

or Professor Weiss, not just a little old man everyone calls
Zayde and no one really listens to. Who knows?"

"It's not fair!"

"No, it's not. But a lot of people miss out on the life that
would have suited them best."

"What do you mean?"

"I'm not really sure." She wondered whether she ought
to burden her son with these kinds of thoughts. She didn't
want to get into the habit of confiding in him too much just
because she was lonely.

"Well, you must have meant something, Mum."

"I was just thinking out loud. Anyhow, it's not a problem
for you, Jacob. You know what you're good at, and other
people recognize that you're good at it, and best of all, you
love doing it. So things shouldn't be too complicated for you.
You'll just go on with your music, and everything else will fit
around it." She paused for a moment, startled to feel a twinge
of envy. "Unfortunately, life's not that simple for everyone.
And even if it is, they're not always as lucky as you are."

"What does luck have to do with it?" he asked peevishly.

"Lots more than you realize. Lots! What if we couldn't
afford to buy a piano and get you lessons because we were
poor like Zayde's parents? What if we lived in wartime, or
lost everything in a flood or some other disaster and had to
move and start over somewhere new? You might have lived
your whole life and never discovered your talent."

"Right. Or I could just get run over by a bus tomorrow,
and then what would be the point of anything? But I'm going
to write music one day. Jewish music. So what do you think
of that?"

"I think that's a wonderful idea," Clara replied, relieved
to drop the topic. "And I also think it's time for bed now.

Tomorrow is Chanukah, you know, and the big party at Aunt Alice's house."

"Latkes, hurrah! I'll bet I can eat more than anyone."

"Not more than Uncle Sidney!" Clara laughed. Her big, comfortable brother-in-law was famous for his appetite.

"No, nobody can eat more than Uncle Sidney," Jacob agreed, giving his mother a hug and going upstairs, whistling the Mendelssohn.

The tailor confessed that he'd been coughing blood for some time. His oldest daughter was getting married next month and he wanted to make a beautiful simcha for her, but he wasn't sure how much longer he could keep hiding his condition from his family. Yes, he did have afternoon fevers, and yes, sometimes he woke up sweating at night. He told his wife it was nightmares. God knows they both had plenty of those.

Ned took out his stethoscope and listened to the man's sunken chest, knowing in advance what to expect. The tailor's wheeze was so loud he had heard him all the way down the hall. He wrote a requisition for an x-ray and sent him down the street in the wake of Mrs. Guttman.

Today was not proving to be a very happy day for the doctor or his patients. Two more to see and then perhaps he'd go for a quick walk in the marshes before dinner. It was relatively mild for December, the rain had let up, and a walk would clear his head, separate the workday from his evening at home. Or no, perhaps not at home, he had to go check on the old lady. Anyhow, it would do him good to ramble a bit along the river Lea. He'd follow the towpath north and then cut across to where the river curved, narrowed, and gathered strength, turning from a placid stream to a potentially dangerous torrent, shallow and full of protruding rocks and roots. He liked the transition it made, showing its other face, where the thickets were wild with rabbits and foxes: a green wilderness in the middle of London. His own heart, hidden and inconsolable, always quickened to the movement of water

After the last patient had gone, he said goodbye to Miss Salmon, briskly bundling the sheets from the examination room. For a moment he lingered in the doorway as if today they might exchange more than formalities. Miss Salmon was the only woman he'd ever met who was entirely unmoved by his charm, and her impassive demeanour had started to unnerve him. He had begun to think that she was not only impervious to him but actively disliked him. She was always prompt, efficient, and polite. But surely there had to be more to her than her job. Surely he had to be more to her than just an employer.

However, she kept on with her tasks, ignoring his increasingly obvious invitation, so he went upstairs to pull on his boots and tell Mother not to wait for him for dinner. Mrs. Abraham was in the sitting room listening to Brahms's Double Concerto; she nodded her head in perfunctory greeting and then waved him away in time to the music with one bony hand.

Ned's mother had never been talkative. Chops or omelette? Bach or Handel? were the main topics of discussion in their household, although sometimes she would ask him about his work and become interested in a particular patient or problem. She had a great appetite for scientific facts. On other occasions, usually around Jewish holidays, she would reminisce about her childhood in Russia and all the family she had lost.

By mutual consent, neither of them mentioned his father.

It only got noisy when Alta came to visit. Luckily, his sister lived a very busy life in Manchester and wasn't able to get away much. She was constantly inviting them to stay with her, especially Mama: wouldn't she like to see her grandchildren more often? They were growing so fast she would hardly recognize them.

Mrs. Abraham usually found an excuse not to travel: her hip, the weather even, though Ned was not aware of this, poor Neddie, who works too hard and doesn't take care of himself. Nevertheless, two or three times a year she would pack a case and go by train for a week of laughter, sticky kisses, and endless chatter. Then she'd come home and say, "Well, thank God *that's* over. And now for some peace and quiet." But while she was showing Ned the gifts the children had made for her (a pincushion in the shape of a tomato, an embroidered eyeglass case, a painted wooden frame holding a group photograph), she would sniff away a tear and call herself a silly old woman, and Ned would give her an awkward hug and tell her she should really have stayed longer, she needn't have rushed back. Maybe they'd go together the next long weekend.

Sometimes they did, Ned bracing himself for the inevitable campaign to acquaint him with one or another of his sister's unmarried friends. Somehow, they were always "dropping in" whenever Ned came to Manchester. But when he confronted Alta about one too many such accidental meetings, she just laughed and said that since he wouldn't take the time to find a suitable girl, it was her responsibility to do it for him.

Where she discovered these eligible young ladies was something of a mystery, since she was six years older than Ned and frantically busy with the activities of her five children and an impressive array of women's charities. But his sister was the kind of capable soul who always seemed able to fit in another obligation. Ned sometimes joked that the reason he hadn't married was that she had scared him out of it: he didn't want anyone to organize *him*. Other times, he said that no one could live up to his sister's example. Both half-truths, as the siblings recognised.

Alta's firm warm hand enclosed his smaller one on the first day of school. He leaned into her body, smelling the good familiar smell: bread and soap, her gingery hair, and something else, something special, just Alta. He looked down at his new shoes. They were so shiny! And he had a pencil box, just like the big boys, with a sliding cover. Smooth pale wood, with a picture of a grey and white kitten batting a ball of red wool. Inside there were two pencils sharpened as fine as could be and a pink rubber for making mistakes disappear. He kept sliding the miraculous cover back and forth to survey this treasure, to sniff the spicy wood, the sharp lead, and the sweet rubber. The pencil box was his best thing. Alta gave it to him.

At the bottom of Templar Street, there was a low wall overlooking a beck. They were supposed to stay away from there. That's where the hooligans came over from Mabgate, shouting, "Get the sheenies." Ned must never go there, it was too dangerous. Jackie Etcovitch got hit in the head with a stone and almost lost an eye; his mother went to the police but they didn't do anything. "What's a sheeny?" asked Ned.

"A bad word," said his sister. "Don't let Mama hear you say it."

Alta knew everything. He started school already reciting his letters and numbers because she taught him. He was her precious pet. Mama and Papa were always too busy, so it was Alta who walked him home from school, Alta who played endless games of pitch and patience, Alta who helped with lessons. The eight times table was the hardest, and spelling. "Road," "rowed," and "rode" all sounded the same, but "row" and "row" were sometimes different: "the oarsmen had a row over who could row faster." English was much harder than Yiddish, Papa said. He always kept a dictionary open on the table beside him as he read the newspaper.

Some things Alta couldn't explain, however. For instance, why should God save the King? What should God save the King from? He and the King had the same name, Edward, but nobody in England was named Malka or Chaim; nobody was named Alta, "the old lady." Alta had a special name to fool the evil eye, because the first baby died. Mama and Papa never talked about the first baby; all Ned knew was that she got sick with the same illness that killed Bubbe Sarah, before Mama and Papa came to Leeds.

Sometimes they talked about other people. Ned liked to hear about Uncle Eli, Mama's favourite older brother, who was conscripted by the Cossacks when he was eighteen and never seen again. He had just got married; in the custom of the shtetl, he gave the girl — Goldie was her name — a get just before he left. And a good thing too, because without a formal divorce she could never have married again, poor thing. Ned was named after him, after him and the King. When he turned six, Mama gave him Eli's violin; she brought it all the way to England with her, only the violin and her mother's candlesticks. Everything else she left for her sisters, not that there was much to choose from. Her sister Gittel said they should take their father's Torah for mazel, but Mama said it had brought him nothing but bad luck, so she wouldn't touch it.

After Ned told this story to Reuben Nussbaum, Reuben's mother said he was a little apikoros, a heathen, and wouldn't let Reuben play with him anymore. Mama said never mind, some people are ignorant peasants, you're better off without them. But later he heard her telling Papa what happened, and she was crying. Papa was angry, as usual. Boom, boom, went his voice all night in the next room. Ned pulled the sheet over his head and wished he could still play with Reuben, who was nice and had a lovely set of tin soldiers.

His parents were both like and unlike the other parents in the Leylands. They had the same funny accents and talked Yiddish to each other, though they insisted that he and Alta talk English. They worried about their children's health and were ambitious for their education. Though she looked down on the other mothers (whom she found ignorant and dowdy), Mama still liked to loiter in the market, boasting about how smart Alta was, how neat and helpful, and what a clever little pitseleh Neddie was turning out to be, he could already read English better than she could. Ned and Alta would just stand there, carrying bundles of bread and fish, string bags of carrots and onions, wishing for a penny to buy candy, knowing better than to ask for it.

But after the first year, Ned no longer went to cheder with the other boys after school. The melamed was old and smelly; he smoked cigarettes all the time and made them recite endlessly while he stared out the window. Ned hated it and was happy to have more time to practise violin or just to read peacefully at the kitchen table with Alta until his mother came home from the factory. Anyhow, Alta didn't have to learn Hebrew, so why should he? His mother and father still argued about this at night when they thought he was asleep: "bar mitzvah," Mama would say, and "superstitious nonsense," Papa would reply.

Papa didn't believe in religion. He refused to darken the door of the Beth HaMidrash HaGadol, even to hear Rabbi Daiches, who was supposed to be the most learned man in England. He went bareheaded all the time so everyone would know. Mama wore hats in rain or sun, but she had beautiful hair that she let Ned brush every night before bed. It was long and slippery and a dark shiny brown, and he loved to run his hands down it. It smelled different from Alta's: thicker, like under the blankets. The other mothers covered their heads with kerchiefs or hats all the time; some even wore stiff wigs that sat on their skulls like lampshades. He and Alta used to laugh at them; they called them teapot-heads, and said that their husbands' yarmulkas were the tea cozies.

Clara dropped in a couple of papery bay leaves, a handful of chopped leek, another of thick winter carrots. In the morning she had made an apple cake; tonight she'd washed the children's hair. Except for Jacob, who'd been outfitted for his piano recital, they might look a bit shabby, but they'd do. Evvie at least had new shoes, cheerful red leather, with bows. She was extremely proud of them, keeping them right by her bed so she could admire them first thing in the morning, last thing at night.

What remained to be done? When Millie came in the morning to do the cleaning, she could iron the dresses, but Clara preferred to wrap the children's presents herself. Little bags of almonds, raisins, and chocolate coins, and one book apiece, so they wouldn't feel too envious of their friends' lavish presents from Father Christmas.

It was always so hard to maintain the balance, so hard not to be *too* different. To be English first. To nod and smile at the well-meaning "Merry Christmas" on everyone's lips and say "Thank you, and the same to your family" a hundred, a thousand times, and never object. To explain calmly to Evvie why she couldn't have a Christmas stocking, why they didn't have a tree. To avoid books with gorgeous illustrations depicting the holiday as a child's paradise. A paradise her own children could not enter.

Alice's youngest granddaughter, Pearl, was too small for books but might still enjoy getting a gift, or at least unwrapping it. Clara had made her a set of building bricks out of colourful squares of fabric, stuffed with kapok. Evvie had been very keen on these, picking out all the scraps and matching them to different colours of yarn for the binding. It had been a happy project for rainy afternoons, though it brought back ambivalent memories of the war years.

Back then, Alice spent a lot of time lying on the settee in her lilac silk dressing gown, a damp tea towel draped over her eyes. Since her husband Sidney had been sent to the front, her migraines had become an almost daily event. So Clara, who was very bored, often minded her little niece and nephew. Anything to get away from the incessant litany of complaint that passed for conversation between her mother and her sister.

"What colour is this, Bernie?" Clara would ask, holding up a sliver of green cloth.

"G'een!"

"And this?"

"Boo!"

"Say blue, moppet. B-loo."

"Boo!" came the inevitable response. And she'd gather him up and tickle him until Mama would say, "Zoll zein sha! You're getting the child too excited before bed," and Alice would complain that her head was just splitting, did anyone have an aspirin?

Then Mama would sweep Bernard up and deposit him firmly in his cot, and they would settle down to some serious work knitting blankets for the Belgian refugees, mufflers and socks for Our Boys at the Front. Clara hated the rough worsted and was not a patient knitter. She much preferred making dolls' clothes and toys. Mama showed her how to make the bricks, cutting the squares out evenly and edging them with blanket stitch. She made twenty, a dazzle of colours and patterns that she and Bernard built into towers and bridges, then smashed down amidst great gales of laughter.

Sometimes her brother Arthur would join the game, to Bernard's delight. He would do anything to get Arthur's attention but usually failed. Arthur was too old for babies, too young for the war. Thank God! said Mama, whose nerves were frayed ever since her oldest boy, Jacob, had signed up on his nineteenth — and last — birthday. A little more light went out of her every day that Jake was gone. Young Arthur was the only one of them whose spirits were irrepressible.

When they tried to keep him indoors, he stayed glued to the wireless, following every campaign, talking of nothing but trenches and whiz-bangs and no man's land and what he, personally, would do to the Hun. He marched around, shouldering a broom for a bayonet and bellowing,

> *Come on and join, come on and join*
> *Come on and join Lord Kitchener's army.*
> *Ten bob a week, plenty grub to eat,*
> *Bloody great boots make blisters on yer feet*

with Bernard following behind, screaming "Bang, bang, bang," until Mama asked him to stop, please, her heart was breaking. Papa kept out of everything down at the bakery, struggling with reduced staff and inferior flour. People still had to eat, he said, even in wartime. Essential service, bread.

In those days they lived for the post. Usually Jake's letters were funny, full of a solder's mad humour, hinting at horror but never requiring that those back home actually imagine it. He preferred to joke about which would be tastier, stewed boots or bully beef, or which quieter, Clara's chatter or the German artillery fire. But once he was at the front, all they received were field service postcards that revealed nothing. Nothing of where or how or even who he was. Nothing at all.

NOTHING is to be written on this side except the date and signature of the sender. Sentences not required may be erased. <u>If anything else is added the post card will be destroyed.</u>

I am quite well.
I have been admitted into hospital
$\begin{Bmatrix} \text{sick} \\ \text{wounded} \end{Bmatrix}$ and am going on well.
and hope to be discharged soon.

I am being sent down to the base.

I have received your
$\begin{Bmatrix} \text{letter dated} \rule{3cm}{0.4pt} \\ \text{telegram } " \rule{3cm}{0.4pt} \\ \text{parcel } " \rule{3cm}{0.4pt} \end{Bmatrix}$

Letter follows at first opportunity.

I have received no letter from you
$\begin{Bmatrix} \text{lately} \\ \text{for a long time.} \end{Bmatrix}$

Signature $\Big\}$
only.
Date \rule{4cm}{0.4pt}

The last one they received was signed and dated June 30, 1916. Everything was crossed out except "I am quite well." The taciturn formality of the postcard was almost as bad as the blue telegram that was to follow it, its evil twin. Both were not-Jacob. Never Jacob anymore.

Luckily, the Armistice came before Arthur was old enough to fight. But they lost him anyway to Canada, where he became an important person in a Montreal bank, sailing home only for weddings and funerals. Since the crash, he couldn't even do that; Clara hadn't seen her wayward brother for years. She had no one but Alice now, of all her family. She who had always been the little one, with so many others to care for her, now had to take care of her own children all by herself.

Clara called upstairs to Jacob to turn off his light, scooped matzo balls out of boiling water. Enough. Maybe she'd write Arthur a letter tonight. He was a very sporadic correspondent, sending one letter for every two or three of hers, but his were wonderful, full of vivid descriptions of French-Canadian nightclubs full of American Negroes playing jazz and Italians and Jews gambling in the back room. It was such a different world where he lived, all those places and peoples mixed up like that! And he had a great talent for capturing dialogue; Mama always said that a letter from Arthur was as good as a trip to the cinema.

Of course, she'd never forgiven him for running away. And when he showed up at Papa's funeral with his wife Marie-Claire, a conspicuous silver crucifix glittering over her conspicuously pregnant belly, Mama had finally been speechless. She'd never forgiven Sidney either, for coming home when Jake didn't. So after Sidney got demobbed, he and Alice moved out, right across town to Hammersmith, and for a while Clara hardly saw them. They deserved a bit of peace after all that, said Sidney.

Clara not only understood but followed as soon as she married Leonard. He objected at first, but there was a synagogue in Brook Green, and parks and fresh air for all the children they were going to have, and good schools, and wasn't Whitechapel getting too crowded anyway? It wasn't all that far really, he could still go to work at the drapery and his father could visit them for Shabbes dinner.

It had been the right decision, as much as it had hurt Zayde and of course Clara's own mother, not having children and grandchildren right next door. They'd been free — truly free — for the first time in their lives. Except when her parents came to visit, there was no one to check up on her housekeeping or to scrutinize her husband's manners. No one to tell them they ought not to sit on the wet grass and make a supper of apples, their very own wet grass and their own apples too! And she had a ceanothus in her front yard, bluer almost than she could bear, bluer than sea or sky, a new country in and of itself. And a lovely old rose clambered up the brick wall in the back, and geese flew over, V for victory, on their way to the reservoir in Barnes.

She wiped her hands on a dishcloth and climbed up to Jacob's room. He was already asleep, the covers pulled over his head so that only the tousled crown showed. She folded the sheet down gently and kissed a hot cheek, put a bookmark in the volume he'd been reading and placed it on his dresser. Next door Danny had kicked off his quilt, while Evvie was so hemmed in by dolls and teddies and assorted plush animals she could hardly move. Each night was the same; she covered one, uncovered the other, kissed three dark heads, and started shedding garments almost before she reached her own room.

Her shoes sat waiting by the front door, released from

their obligation to take her out into the world. She was no longer someone to be identified by curious passersby, not a redhead, not a Jew. Her apron dangled from a kitchen chair, no one's widow. She unbuttoned her dress, unclipped her hair. No one's daughter, no one's mother. She tossed her slip, brassiere, and knickers on the bed. There were always so many layers to strip away before she could find herself. And pouring a cap-full of lavender-scented oil into the tumbling water, Clara slid gratefully into the bath.

The grass was withered and muddy, the trees along the tow-path leafless and cold looking. Hackney. The name came from *Hakon Ea*, Hacken's island, in tribute to a Danish settler at the time of King Canute. Just another insignificant piece of dry land between many streams and rivulets. Islands within islands. The whole East End was an island of Yiddish-speakers within an island of English-speakers within an island of other languages: Scots, Irish, Welsh, and Cornish.

A family of coots swam along the water's edge, honking like bicycle horns. Their comical white bills shovelled under floating rafts of scum for a late dinner. Watching them, Ned suddenly remembered the body in the Thames three or four weeks ago. Day after day he'd scrutinized the newspapers for any mention, however fleeting, of the drowned man, but there was nothing. Surely he had to be someone's father or someone's husband? Unless he had been a recent immigrant fleeing the Nazis; there were more of those people every day, people no one wanted. After all, the word "refugee" was close kin to the word "refuse."

Ned shivered. He had walked as quickly as possible across

69

the marshes to chase the chill from his bones, but now that the sun had gone down, it was getting really cold and starting to rain again. Best walk back, dry off, and have dinner. Some of these days were just too long.

By the time he got home, Mother had eaten and was back in her chair, at work on a piece of petit point. Thank goodness her eyesight was still sharp. After she quit Coates Burton in Leeds to come down to London with Ned, she started a little business of her own, doing needlework handbags, chair covers, and fire screens for some of the fancier shops. It kept her busy, she said, and they could use the extra money. His mother had never been able to sit idle for long. Her hands moved swiftly over rococo scenes of topiary and fountains, ladies in ringlets and flounces, rosy cherubs and lapdogs. A fantasy world executed in tiny shimmering threads. When he was small, Ned had loved to go through her embroidery box, sorting the floss into a rainbow: red, orange, yellow, green, blue, indigo, and violet. He never knew where to put the pink threads, though — at the beginning or the end? — until one day he realised he could join the colours in a circle.

Ned ate his dinner quickly, then decided to bathe and change before heading to the hospital. Later, he wondered if he had intuited how long a night it would be, if somehow he knew Mrs. Guttman was not going to make it. At the time, he simply felt tired and in need of cleansing. When he finally got home four hours later, after consoling the sobbing Mrs. Schwartz, her three silent black-hatted brothers, and the sister who arrived too late from Bristol, he undressed without turning on the light, slipped between cool sheets. Sleep came quickly: a dark curtain. He dreamed of Mrs. Guttman floating down the Thames with a teapot on her head.

Spring – Summer 1935

Spring

January and February were unusually cold. Jacob walked to school glumly, his satchel thumping against his legs, coming home chilled and argumentative. Evvie and Danny, cooped up inside, became increasingly rowdy. Clara found herself asking Millie to look after them more and more often so she could go for a walk alone, striding quickly as she never could with their short legs stumbling alongside and their shrill voices complaining. In summer she had the patience to stop every few feet to count the aphids on a rose or to watch an ant's progress under a single grain of rice, but not now. She wanted to march out her frustrations all by herself and then come home to a nice cup of tea and a lapful of affection.

For her part, Millie was happy to do anything that got her away from chores. She was an ineffectual housekeeper at best but so sweet-natured Clara didn't have the heart to let her go. The children loved her because she indulged them in every way. She spooned the plumpest strawberries from the jam, placing one on each scone. Her crumpets dripped butter; her cinnamon toast glittered with sugar. She even wrapped cheese sandwiches in a clean towel and filled old lemonade bottles with water for them to carry off to a desert island. With Millie in charge, Evvie piled the sitting room cushions into castles or draped chairs with sheets to make Indian tents for hours of make-believe. Danny tried to help but usually knocked everything down, which led to tears of wrath on Evvie's part and tears of remorse and frustration on his. Then Millie, displaying remarkably little reluctance, wasted most of the afternoon rebuilding their ephemeral constructions instead of doing the laundry and barely had time to put everything to rights and get supper on the stove before she had to leave.

So when the children were with her, Clara usually encouraged more orderly pursuits like drawing or pasting cut-outs in an album or listening to stories. They brought piles of books home from their weekly trip to the library, mostly fairytales, with delicate watercolour illustrations of Aladdin rubbing his magic lamp and an enormous Genie billowing out like blue smoke, the Snow Queen carrying off a sleepy boy in her thrilling chariot of ice, Red Riding Hood knocking on the cottage door as the wolf, in a frilly lace cap, bared yellow fangs from Grandma's bed.

They had an unquenchable appetite for disaster, these little ones, as long as conclusive reversals followed. One rainy March afternoon, Jacob, half-listening as he doodled away at some music theory, suddenly had a revelation.

"They're all in sonata form, Mum."

"What are?"

She had just reached the part when Hansel offers the witch a scrawny chicken bone instead of his chubby finger, and Danny (who had to be the boy in every tale) was clutching Evvie (who was always the girl) with an enthusiastic combination of terror and delight.

"Fairytales. They all start off happy. Then the adventure

begins and there's a new key, that's the sad or scary part. And then it all comes right in the end. Happy, sad, happy — major key, minor key, major key."

"Hmm. Perhaps. But what about Hans Christian Anderson? Some of his stories end so miserably. Like 'The Little Mermaid' or 'The Steadfast Tin Soldier' or worst of all, 'The Red Shoes.' Imagine chopping off a little girl's feet to punish her for vanity!"

"Whose feet get chopped off, Mama?" Only two and a half, Danny was tantalised by violence.

"Only in a story, pet. No one real," Clara replied. "It's just a story."

"Read that one!"

"Maybe another time. We already started a new book today,"

"Finish it *now*, Mama," said Evvie. "Let's get to when the witch goes in the oven. That's my favourite part."

"Well, there are some sonatas that go sad, happy, sad, but I don't like those as well either," Jacob remarked. Experience had taught him that nobody could finish a conversation around Evvie and Danny unless he forged ahead, right over every bump and detour.

"Everyone loves a happy ending," said Clara. "Now that spring's finally coming, we think of the nice weather as the way it ought to be and winter as just an in-between part."

And spring *was* finally coming. First it was nothing but a rumour. The rain fell as coldly as ever on the naked arms of trees, and nothing stirred in the dull mud of a thousand stalled gardens. But one day there was a softness, a faint green haze at twig-tip. Birds sang earlier and preened shiny wet feathers on the lawn. Lawns themselves looked a little warmer, a little richer. Worms coiled on grass that bent and swayed, unburdened by frost. And a buoyancy entered everyone's step; even their dour milkman whistled as he lined up the shining glass bottles — one, two, three — under the crabapple tree.

In Clara's garden, brilliant blue scilla flowed through the grass; crocuses unfurled peach and cream and purple stripes; birds strutted and sang, flaunting their courting plumage. The children became fascinated by bugs, turning over every stone to see what wakened, what squirmed, what crawled. They filled jars with specimens and demanded that Clara look them all up in the library, then label each container with both Latin and English names. Danny and Evvie learned the difference between spiders and insects, moths and butterflies. The fairy stories were abandoned. Real creatures that really flew had usurped their interest.

Mostly Jacob stayed indoors, practising the piano. His concert was scheduled for May. Any day now he would have to meet with that serious-looking doctor and play for him. Miss Westerham seemed to feel he was good enough, but Jacob wasn't sure. How could Mozart have composed this piece when he was even younger than Jacob? Mozart was a genius, of course, and he was not, but still . . . He could see his whole life stretching out ahead of him, years and years of never writing anything as good as the music Mozart wrote when he was only ten.

His mother was impatient with this premature despair. She was forever digging in the compost or starting seedlings in a pot or dividing perennials. The house spilled over with catalogues and seed packets and smelled of wet earth. When the children came down for breakfast only Millie would be in the kitchen, singing as she stirred the porridge. Clara was already in the garden, wearing an old shirt of their father's, spearing dandelions or killing slugs. Sometimes she leaned on her spade, daydreaming, or sat peacefully sipping a steaming mug of tea. But mostly she worked until the sweat ran down her face, moving plants around, making room for new specimens. Another clematis for the south-facing wall, or perhaps this year she'd try an espaliered pear.

"Your mother's gone mad, I think," said Millie. "She makes more work for herself than that wee bit of garden can hold!"

"Mama loves flowers," said Evvie loyally.

"Of course, darling. And who doesn't?" Millie replied, giving the girl an affectionate pat on the head. "I meant no offence, surely."

"She's getting ready for our father's yahrzeit," remarked Jacob. "You know, the anniversary of his death. It's next week. We're going to light candles in the garden and say a prayer there."

"Are you now? Well, isn't that a beautiful idea. We put a lilac on my gran's grave after she died, and I always said I wanted the same someday myself. Flowering trees last such a long time. Longer than memory, sometimes."

"We have a lilac," said Danny. "It smells purple."

"Purple is a colour, you silly," declared Evvie. "It doesn't have a smell."

"It does so!" Danny started to cry. "Mama said."

"Your mother is right, and so are you," Millie said. "Now eat your porridge."

The big clock in the hall read ten to four. Ned flipped through some sheet music impatiently; he hated waiting but had arrived earlier than anticipated. Too many memories were associated with years and years of waiting in halls like this, hearing muffled sounds of other people practising behind rows of closed doors. Somewhere a flute laughed, a cello moaned; the old windows in their warped frames vibrated to a timpani's steady thud. He closed his eyes and leaned his head against the damp, peeling wallpaper.

Back in Leeds, there had been a time when he tried to arrive early for music, to sit near Lucy Chadwick and watch her sharp white teeth bite into the red apple she invariably brought with her. Ivory teeth. Neat little bites like struck keys. Her piano lesson took place right across the hall from his violin class with the imperious Mr. Nash. But whereas Ned always arrived dishevelled (shirt untucked, boots scuffed), Lucy was the cleanest-looking person he had ever seen. Her nails were shining white moons and her hands spotless. She even smelled like rain.

Ned's mother was extremely well groomed, but there was something counterfeit about her appearance. Maybe it was that he knew how much effort it cost for her to be fashionable: the haggling at the draper's over each yard of stuff, the late nights sitting up over a pattern, the painstaking hand-stitching. But Lucy just sat there, fresh as the dawn of Creation, fair hair knife-edged and shining, eating her apple round and round. Her method fascinated Ned. She always finished with a symmetrically shaped core, which she held by the stem and popped back in her paper bag. Then she folded down the edge of the bag, ran a clean white finger along the edge to sharpen the fold, and dropped it in the dustbin.

Lucy seemed able to concentrate on one thing at a time and therefore to do it perfectly. But for Ned the world drifted, full of conflicting enticements. So he munched apples absent-mindedly, spitting out the seeds, the sharp membrane at the centre caught between his teeth. Even in school it was his quick-wittedness, not his concentration, that saw him through. From the tail end of a teacher's query, echoing behind the sound of his own name, he could usually reconstruct the whole question and answer it. Lucy's apples became an inspiration to sharpen his attention: to do only one thing at a time and to do it properly. Even now he thought of the sun as an apple that rose each day anew to be eaten neatly round the core.

Lucy became aware of his attention and smiled back shyly. Soon he started to bring apples, eating them in her methodical fashion. And after several weeks of companionable apple-eating, they began going for walks, first around the building and then outdoors in fair weather, meeting earlier and earlier. Sometimes they were actually late for their music lessons, running in apologetic and out of breath, having wandered too far, deep in conversation.

What did they talk about? Ned can't even remember. All he recalls is the spontaneity of their exchanges, something new to him, who had been raised to scrutinize his every thought, to speak in accordance with the right motives and values or prepare to be cross-examined. At home, every conversation was a minefield. With Lucy, such caution was not required; he was free to sound silly, to contradict himself, to speculate without fear of reproach. She was a sweet soul, without prejudice or rancour, and as sensitive as he was.

But Lucy's teacher must have said something to Lucy's mother, who suddenly appeared, glamorous but unyielding, at the music school one day. They sat together across the hall from Ned, who heard the mother murmur, as she straightened, one by one, the soft kid fingers of her gloves, that Lucy should have nothing more to do with that shabby little Jew.

Within weeks, their relationship was severed. Mrs. Chadwick changed Lucy's lesson to another time, and he never saw her again. When his father disappeared a year later, Ned was better prepared for that loss than he had been for his first, the loss of Lucy.

"Dr. Abraham?" called a tentative young voice. Lucy? Ned opened his eyes with a start and saw not the distant bright angel of his dream but Jacob Weiss, rumpled, dark and boyish.

"Oh, how are you, Jacob? Excuse me, I must have nodded off." He checked his watch. "I got here a bit early, and Miss Westerham hasn't opened her door yet."

"Well, sometimes she's late. But I don't mind," Jacob hastened to add, "because she gives me extra time whenever that happens. She's very nice, Miss Westerham."

"You're lucky. A nice teacher makes music much more fun. My first teacher, Mr. Nash, really, he suited his name. He used to rap me across the knuckles with his baton when he got annoyed. And he got annoyed very easily."

"Really?" said Jacob, horrified. "Miss Westerham would *never* hit anybody!"

"No, I doubt she would. Music makes her happy. But some people have higher expectations, I guess, or are more easily disappointed."

"Is there a difference?"

"That's a good question. I'd have to think about it more to be able to answer you," said Ned, laughing.

"Well, I suppose you could have low expectations and still be disappointed all the time, like the Latin master at my school. He thinks we're all idiots. He expects everyone to make stupid mistakes, but he's still cross when we do."

"There you go, then."

"But could you have high expectations of people and not be easily disappointed?"

"I suppose so. If the people around you were terribly talented."

"Or if you just thought they were. Like my mother. She thinks we're all geniuses."

"You mean you're not? Then I've been misinformed, my good sir, and I believe we should cancel our rehearsal."

Jacob burst out laughing, hugely relieved that this severe-looking man was kind after all. He hoped the music would go well and they would become friends. Just then the door opened. A chubby blond girl trotted out, clutching her mother's hand, and Miss Westerham's deep contralto boomed, "Come in, come in! Let's get started, gentlemen."

Jacob picked up his music, Ned his violin, and they entered her big, untidy studio. It was very hot, and the dusty windows bloomed with an amazing collection of African violets. Miss Westerham wore a tight-fitting purple tweed suit, which gave rather more emphasis than was attractive to her ample behind. Nonplussed by the sight of her and by the jungly smell of the violets, Ned momentarily forgot why he had come.

"Shall we dive right in?" the woman was asking, "or would you rather talk about the piece first? How do you find the Rondeau? I've always found it a bit disappointing in a way. The Adagio is so unforgettable, but I can never keep the second movement in my head."

"Perhaps we should play it first and see what we've each

discovered on our own," Ned suggested. "I'm sure we'll find lots to talk about when we put the parts together."

"How is that with you, Jacob?" Miss Westerham asked the boy.

Jacob was so nervous he just nodded. If he could only get to the piano, Mozart would rescue him, throw him a net of triplets flowing one over the other, hand over hand, and he wouldn't have to speak at all.

Soon they were deep in the music, all three. Could they be hearing the same thing? Science has determined that the frequency of middle C is precisely 256 vibrations per second, but sensation alone is not meaning. To Jacob, middle C was home, the place you start from, safe haven. Even on the page it resembled a smiling face or a sun. But on Ned's violin, the note had no special status. It was one of many gradations of sound, one colour in the rainbow. He did not orient himself from or to it; to him, there was no middle, for he did not see the notes laid out in a row. He felt for them along an infinite scale of possibility.

Miss Westerham, watching them, was struck — not for the first time — by the differences instruments elicit in those who play them. Violinists were swimmers, she felt, pulling and pushing the water back and forth with their arms and shoulders. They were inside the sound; it was their element. Pianists were more like climbers, scrabbling up a mountain whose peak glinted above the clouds like a mirage. Or maybe it was just a matter of scale, the violin being so small, warm, and mammalian, nestled beside the chin, the piano glittering black and white, slate and marble, dwarfing whoever sat at it.

But at the same time, the piano was bright and the violin

dark, befitting their vintage. Innocence and experience, the mind oblivious to limit while the body sways under its own weight. And the contrast between the two was emphasized by the piece the man and boy were playing together: K30, the Sonata in F major, the keyboard part beautifully lyrical and at the same time energetic, the violin melancholy and restrained, anticipating each modulation to the minor.

Miss Westerham listened, enthralled. The meaning of the piece had never been so clear to her before, and she felt sure that the audience at the spring concert would see it the way she did; it was as lucid as reading the score. And she would have her triumph. For in spite of her lumpy figure and her garish wardrobe, Miss Westerham had her pride. She knew well enough how Dr. Abraham saw her, and she knew well enough how he saw a beautiful woman like Magda Tabori. She did feel a small pang at what she had missed out on in life and a greater one at how misprized her real accomplishments were. But she could tell from Ned's increasing excitement that she would make a convert of him, perhaps even a friend, and that her chief concern, Jacob's talent, would be cherished.

"How did it go, Jacob?" his mother asked, distracted. Millie was just clearing away the last of the dinner things, more frantically than usual because it was late, while Danny kept shrieking from upstairs, wanting a story.

"It was smashing. Dr. Abraham's really friendly and easy to talk to, not stuck-up like we thought, and the piece sounds much better once you add in the violin. I felt a bit embarrassed, though, because my part is bigger than his."

"Isn't it called a sonata for violin *and* piano?" Clara couldn't imagine that haughty man allowing himself to be upstaged by a little boy.

"Well, actually, when it was first published it said 'for keyboard, with violin accompaniment.' Because Mozart's instrument was the piano, you know. Maybe he wasn't as good on violin."

"Stop whining, Mr. Daniel, I'm almost ready. Goodbye Millie, and thank you. We'll see you in the morning," said Clara. "Jacob, I'd love to hear more about your rehearsal, but you can see it's bedlam around here right now. Why don't you eat your dinner, and we'll talk after I get these two monkeys off to bed?"

"Jakey, Jakey, I want a kiss!" Evvie yelled down the stairs.

"Jakey, Jakey!" echoed Danny.

For weeks now this scene had repeated itself. The friendly colloquy in the hall, the intense, almost wordless, practice session, the return to frenzied domesticity. Jacob lost interest in discussing the piece with his mother; he preferred the ambience of Miss Westerham's studio. And he started to look forward to his abbreviated discussions with Dr. Abraham, who was serious, as Jacob had suspected, but not pompous. He treated Jacob with respect, or so it seemed. In any event, he didn't tousle his hair or call him Jakey or make patronizing comments like most of the other adults Jacob knew.

Jacob had always talked avidly with Miss Westerham, but their conversations were largely pragmatic. What is the feeling in this passage, how slow is andante, how much slower largo? But with Dr. Abraham he found himself moving towards the kind of speculations he once shared with his father.

When Papa had died he had not yet found words for all the hummings and yearnings inside him. Still, even then, there had been nights in the garden when they'd looked up at the stars and talked of where we come from, what happens after death, how the universe starts and if it ends. Now he found himself touching on those issues again, through the Mozart, and was delighted to discover that Dr. Abraham seemed to understand exactly what he was feeling.

Perhaps because he was a doctor, Ned was very good at teasing out nuances of feeling from people, making them eloquent in spite of themselves, prodding them towards clarity. Where exactly is the pain, and what kind of pain is it: sharp and sudden or a slow burn, a nagging ache or a blow that makes you dizzy and sick? Is it the kind of pain that stops your breath, the kind you forget about till it flares, the kind that grows and grows until everything outside of you is muffled and distant and the pain inhabits your every nerve and the only way you can imagine it ending is by ending yourself?

Jacob adored such fine discriminations when they were transferred to the world of his own interests. His mother didn't have the time or inclination for splitting hairs, but at eleven, he had all the time in the world. It was part of the discipline of his Hebrew classes as well, and though some of the boys scoffed and stared out the window and passed notes, it seemed to Jacob terribly urgent that one be accurate, always, about everything.

These days, his mother seemed so sloppy to him. He was embarrassed when she met him at school, Danny squirming in the pushchair, covered in biscuit crumbs, Evvie hiding behind Clara's skirt, sucking her thumb, Clara's hair a carroty frizz, her hem coming down. Once she'd even had a big blob of raspberry jam on her sleeve. Dr. Abraham's nails were always better manicured than hers were, even though he was a man, and this seemed significant to Jacob. His mother had let her life get out of control.

It was important to keep in control, Jacob thought. That's what music was about, after all: themes and variations, melody taken through every possible translation but always brought back to its origin, never quite escaping. Repetition almost to the point of tedium, and then the reprieve.

"But ordinary life is like that too, Jakey," Clara objected when, in his own halting way, he finally confided some of these thoughts to her. "I know it's like that for me. Most of my days are so repetitive. Sometimes I simply cannot bear the thought of making another meal or reading another story or mending another shirt. It becomes pure drudgery. But then there's a shift — Danny says something funny, or it finally stops raining and the boring lunch becomes a picnic, or the story I'm reading turns out to be one I've never read before and really like. And then everything's new again."

"Not everything, Mum." Jacob laughed sardonically, a new tone with him and not one Clara liked. "You still have to make that meal or mend that shirt."

"Well, you still have to practise the piano, but you don't get tired of it."

"I do, sometimes."

"We all get tired of what we have to do sometimes. But constant novelty would be just as tiring, maybe worse. Imagine having to begin a new piece every day. Just think about it. Wouldn't starting over every single time be worse than trying to improve the pieces you were already working on? Wouldn't it be more frustrating to never finish anything properly, to keep flitting from one project to the next? I want my flowers to come up in the same spot every year and not to switch places underground just to surprise me. Even so, it's never the same garden. Some plants do beautifully, others give in to disease or age, and some need to be pruned radically. It's repetition with variation, just as you said."

Jacob nodded, lost somewhere in his mother's metaphors. Once he found himself agreeing with her, he forgot his original point. But he still felt dissatisfied with Clara and hemmed in by the clutter and noise of his home. For the first time, he had begun to think of growing up as a goal. He began to look forward to his *own* life. He might do what Dr. Abraham had done, become something sensible like a doctor while continuing to play music for pleasure. This seemed to him quite an accomplishment, to do two things at once. Clara, on the other hand, had done nothing with her life; she just took care of children. And yet she knew quite a lot, read tons of books, painted beautifully. It was a waste, really.

Of course, he could never say such things to his mother, but he did, hesitantly, to Dr. Abraham, who replied that, to be frank, domesticity had never held much interest for him.

"But don't you want to get married?" Jacob asked.

"Why?" Ned replied, taken aback by the boy's directness. Was there no one who would spare him this inquisition?

"Because everybody gets married, don't they? I mean, to have a family, children — you know, ordinary life."

"It depends, I suppose, if you want to be ordinary," Ned countered. "Some of us don't feel the need. Quite a lot of artists and musicians, scientists too, all kinds of great thinkers have never married. It takes a lot of time, marriage, especially if there are children. Some people prefer to spend their time working."

"Is that how you feel? That there's no time for anything but work?"

"For me, yes. I couldn't possibly be a good doctor as well as a good musician if I had to take care of a family too. Or not as good as I'm capable of being. And I wouldn't be happy being anything less than that."

This was a new thought to Jacob. Sometimes, these days, he felt like he would burst from too many new thoughts. The familiar boundaries of his childhood world had been shattered with the death of his father. He already knew that life wasn't safe; now, too many other assumptions were being challenged. Maybe his mother wasn't right about everything, maybe she didn't understand as much about the world as he had thought. But Dr. Abraham knew a lot. He actually travelled. Every year he went to Vienna once or twice to see his violin teacher, and then he went somewhere else as well: Paris or Florence or Venice or Rome. He'd even been as far as Athens and gone on a walking tour of all those famous ruins. Of course he knew better than Mum did. Where had she ever gone? She barely even left the stupid house! She hardly even bothered to brush her stupid hair!

Jacob immediately felt guilty for thinking this way about his mother, who was kind and funny and worked so hard. Dr. Abraham was kind to him too, and sometimes he even made jokes. But it wasn't the same, really. Nobody could love him the way his mother did. Remorseful, he would go up to Clara, putting his arms around her waist and squeezing his face into her shoulder blade until she cried out, "Jacob, please, my hands are full, you're going to knock me over!" And then he would stomp off to his room, strangely satisfied by the unfairness of it all.

Opening the Door for Elijah

The spring concert at the Guildhall was only two weeks away, but preparations for Passover had eclipsed all other concerns in the Weiss household. The house had to be purged of the slightest crumb of flour in remembrance of the Israelites' flight from Egypt, when they had no time to let their bread rise. Danny ran around with a feather duster, tickling Evvie, while Clara and Millie scrubbed and polished and packed. Whatever could not be eaten in time was sold to Millie for a penny. Some things, like their big bag of oatmeal, she would return after the holiday, but she was glad enough to keep the remainder.

Jacob's Hebrew class was discussing the larger meaning of these domestic rituals. In Egypt the Jews were slaves. Once they were liberated, they were free not only to act but also to err, not only to choose but also to choose wrongly. For a free man, his teacher contended, every week is the week before Pesach; every day we are required to recognize impurities in ourselves and to cleanse them. Every day we must put our house in order.

Jacob found himself listening to his Hebrew teacher with more interest these days. Although he still resented being cooped up through the lengthening afternoons while the shouts of children at play floated through the open window, he was starting to find such discussions meaningful rather than tedious. At school, they were always memorizing and being tested; they were told to be quiet and listen. But at cheder they were encouraged to speak out and even to argue with the teacher about what one ought to do in situations that might arise in everyday life. Sometimes he brought his Hebrew school problems home, admittedly with mixed success. The finer points of debate were generally lost on his siblings.

"Evvie, I've got a question for you."

"Is it a hard one?"

"Not too hard. And it's interesting. Will you try?"

"All right. If you want me to."

"Here it is then. Pay attention, will you?" Somehow her thumb had found her mouth. Evvie's contentedly dazed look suggested that solving moral dilemmas wasn't high on her list of priorities.

"I *am* paying attention. Sucking my thumb helps me think."

"All right, then. Suppose I borrow a book from the library. And suppose you pick it up to look at it and accidentally rip out one of the pages. Who is responsible for the damage, you or me?"

"I wouldn't take your book without asking, Jakey."

"Yes, you would. You do it all the time."

"No, I don't." Her voice rose to a wail of protest, and tears spilled down her cheeks.

"Never mind, Evvie, I'm not accusing you of anything. It's a problem from cheder. Just listen. *I* took out the book, right?

So I've promised to take care of it. But you're the one who ripped it, not me. So who has to pay the library?"

"I can't, 'cause I don't have any money."

"Oh, never mind, you're hopeless. Anyway, I wasn't trying to upset you, you little baby, just teaching you how to think."

In spite of his misgivings, Ned had become fond of Jacob and was really enjoying their Mozart sessions. The boy approached music with an intellectual curiosity that was refreshing. He saw it as fun in a way that Ned had never been able to recapture since his own disappointment with the Leeds symphony. Maybe it was because the Mozart itself was such boyish music, but Ned felt a kind of lightening of the spirit when they played together that lasted all the way home and came back to him in restorative flashes during the long days at work.

And it wasn't just the musical collaboration that made him happy, though Miss Westerham insisted that was going better than she could ever have hoped. There really did seem to be a special affinity between him and Jacob. They both possessed a spiritual hunger for which music was a form of sustenance. Ned couldn't quite understand it or explain it to himself — after all, he was twenty years older than the lad — but he felt it, and he knew Jacob did also. For while they were waiting for Miss Westerham to open her door, the boy revealed himself with such candour he disarmed Ned of his usual reticence. Jacob was lonely; he was angry; he missed his father so much. How could there be a God who let fathers die?

What was the point of anything? He wasn't sure he wanted to be as serious about music as everyone expected him to be, but he was afraid he'd never be good at anything else. He hated school, but he was miserable at home. His mother worried about everything, and his little brother and sister drove him mad wanting attention all the time. He thought Millie was pretty, but that was wrong, wasn't it? She was only a servant, and she wasn't even Jewish, so how could he like her?

None of these revelations was sordid or even unexpected, but they burst from Jacob with the vehemence of long suppression. As a doctor, Ned was used to his patients unburdening themselves, though usually he only listened with half an ear as he took a pulse or tested reflexes. The words streamed past, and he attended only to those details relevant to his diagnosis. But with Jacob it was different. He wasn't just tolerating the boy's confessions out of a sense of duty; he actually cared. And what was more unexpected was that, in listening to Jacob and trying to respond to him honestly, Ned was learning things about himself. It was during one of their conversations that he finally recognized that he hated being Jewish not because there was anything contemptible in his culture, but because other people's contempt made him feel ashamed.

So when Jacob's family asked him to be their guest at the Passover Seder, he accepted. It was easy enough to tell himself he was doing it for Jacob. But if he were honest, he'd have to admit that he was a little curious about Judaism, the religion he'd always rejected as archaic and embarrassing. And there was even a third motivation, more deeply hidden, to do with Clara. Once she'd come to listen to them practice, and when the last note had faded away, instead of clapping she'd come up silently behind her son and kissed the back of his neck. Ned had found himself unaccountably jealous; his stomach hurt from it. For days the intimacy of that gesture, its sweet unselfconsciousness, haunted him. He wanted to be in its presence again.

A maid in a white cap and starched apron came to the door, took his hat and coat, and called "Dr. Abraham is here" in the direction of the drawing room. An older, more florid version of Clara came towards him, flashing diamonds. This must be her sister, Alice Greenbaum, his hostess. A heavy fellow leaning on a cane and wearing a beautifully embroidered waistcoat, a black velvet yarmulke perched on the back of his head, introduced himself as Alice's husband, Sidney. Ned felt momentarily nonplussed. Should he have worn a skullcap too? But they were not in synagogue. And they had invited him knowing full well that he was not observant.

In the large, elegantly appointed drawing room a fire blazed, despite the mild spring weather. A number of children were rolling on a fine Aubusson carpet with a remarkably patient dog. Among them he recognized Evelyn Weiss, Jacob's skinny little sister, who had accompanied her mother to pick up Jacob from music class on one occasion. Then Clara appeared from somewhere, shaking his hand and making introductions: of course he knew her father-in-law, Mr. Weiss, from the Guildhall concert, but he'd never met her youngest child, Daniel, the boy hiding under the grand piano. Yes, it was a Bosendorfer, an exquisite instrument; all the Greenbaum children played beautifully, though not quite at Jacob's level. Sitting on the sofa were the oldest of Alice's sons, Bernard Greenbaum, and his wife Mitzi; their daughter Pearl was the littlest girl on the carpet, soon to be joined by a new brother or sister judging by Mitzi's hugely pregnant belly. Bernard's sister Edna and her husband, Paul Katz, already had a boy and a girl, both fair and freckled and obviously twins. David Greenbaum, dark and belligerent looking, was just home from Oxford for the holiday; the youngest of Alice and Sidney's children, Roger, slouching self-consciously by the window, was still in school.

Ned had never been any good at remembering names; this lot was gone as soon as heard. It was too hot and too many teeth were grinning at him. He regretted more and more that he had come; his head spun from the penetrating smell of lilies and cigars and roast chicken. Luckily Clara was opening a window. And now they must go sit down.

The table shone with silver and sparkled with crystal. There were a great many wineglasses, a great many forks and knives and spoons. He remembered a lot of drinking at these events, and unexpected music. As a child, he had felt a bit left out, not understanding the Hebrew, but he had enjoyed the gaiety and been dumbfounded at the spectacle of his father, who, drawing on hidden reserves of feeling, had sung out the ancient melodies with absolute conviction in his beautiful tenor voice.

They'd gone through the preliminary ritual without incident and were finally enjoying their soup. Clara was proud of her children, Jacob reading the Hebrew flawlessly and the younger two relatively quiet, though curious about the proceedings. Their behaviour was exemplary compared to that of their cousins. Edna sat between her boisterous twins, fairly vibrating with embarrassment. She shushed, smiled, cajoled, teased, and was finally reduced to feeding them little sips of grape juice and bits of matzo to buy silence. The boy, Michael, was surreptitiously dropping matzo into his juice to watch it turn purple before slurping it up more noisily than necessary. Lila, his sister, had built a precarious matzo pyramid. It was hidden from her mother behind the creamy folds of a damask napkin, but Ned, sitting directly opposite, had an unobstructed view of both the twins' activities.

He felt like an observer from another planet. He wondered which of the four sons referred to in the Passover Haggadah he was: the wise son who participates respectfully, the wicked one who rejects his place in the community, the simpleton who bleats out ignorant queries, or the last and least, who doesn't even know what questions to ask. Mostly he noticed that there were a lot of numbers at a seder: four sons, four questions, four glasses of wine; three matzos on the plate; ten plagues. Why was that? Keeping accounts. Counting one's blessings, perhaps.

He recalled "Who knows one?," the numerical game that would conclude the meal, climbing a chromatic scale to the thirteen attributes of God. What were they? Invisibility, inaudibility, incorporeality, inaccessibility, insensitivity, indifference, incompetence . . .

He was glad no one could read his thoughts. He was glad the matzo balls were feathery light; his mother's had always sat like stones in his belly. He was glad they were finally eating. He was very glad Clara was sitting beside him, with her smell of lemons and warm skin, her titian hair glowing in the candlelight. They barely acknowledged each other and yet a current ran between them; a certain distance from the goings-on at the table brought them closer together.

"I don't like this part, Zayde," Evvie exclaimed suddenly, too preoccupied to eat. She pointed to an illustration in her

Haggadah in which huge waves were tumbling the heavily armed Egyptian soldiers, their faces masks of terror.

"They're so frightened. It's not fair. Why does God kill people?"

"God doesn't kill people if they obey him," Alice said impatiently, rubbing lipstick from her water goblet with her thumb. "They were wicked, you know, that's why they had to be punished."

But Zayde replied calmly, "Passover is for answering questions, Alice, and Evvie is a clever girl to ask them. And she's not the only one to worry about those poor Egyptians. The rabbis teach that when we crossed the Red Sea to safety and our enemies could not, we sang a song of thanksgiving. Even the angels in heaven joined in. But Hashem said, 'How can you sing while my children are drowning in the sea?' Do you understand what this means, bubbeleh?"

"God was sorry for the Egyptians?"

"Yes, that's right. So we should be too. This is also why we take a drop of wine out of our glasses for each of the plagues. We make our pleasure less so that we will remember the sufferings of others."

"Frogs, frogs!" shouted Danny, who was trying hard to follow the conversation, though it was already past his bedtime.

"Good boy!" said his mother proudly. "Frogs *were* one of the plagues. You wouldn't like to have frogs hopping all over the house, would you?"

"Yes, I would. I like frogs. Can I have one, Mama?"

"Me too!" shouted Michael, spilling his juice. "A big one."

"We'll see," Clara replied, laughing. "Let's finish our Seder first."

"There's another interpretation of the plagues which may interest you, Dr. Abraham," Zayde continued. He was in his glory tonight, displacing Sidney as the nominal head of the Seder. Sidney did not seem to mind, however, and indulged the old man.

"Yes?" Ned replied politely. Some kind of response seemed to be expected, though it was clear that a lecture was forthcoming regardless.

"You know, Pharaoh was not just an ordinary king. The Egyptians worshipped him as a god, and that's why his advisors were priests. Maybe today we would call them scientists because they did magic and knew how to heal people. In those days, knowledge was power, yes? Not like now, when all you need is weapons. So, these very important priests told Pharaoh not to give in, no matter how horrible the plagues were, because that would mean admitting that the god of a bunch of ignorant slaves was stronger than he was."

"You mean, they couldn't accept the scientific proof before them? If they were real scientists, I doubt it would have taken the deaths of their firstborn to convince them to free the Israelites," said Ned.

Roger, Sidney and Alice's youngest son, laughed loudly; he clearly craved the approval of adults. David, on the other hand, had sulked through the Seder, muttering from time to time under his breath. A storm had been brewing in that direction, and now, as soup bowls were cleared and the adults were murmuring appreciatively over the gefilte fish, its frill of parsley and fin of lemon rind, the red pool of horseradish sauce, while the children looked dubious, the storm broke.

"It's all hypocrisy," he declared, staring at his father in open rebellion.

"David!" Alice reproached him.

Mitzi excused herself and left the room, caressing her enormous belly. She appeared to be reassuring her unborn child rather than her daughter Pearl, who stumbled after her, turning back once to survey the table with puzzled eyes. Bernard, a placid man whose contributions to the reading of the Haggadah had been delivered in a bass monotone, watched the departure of his wife and daughter with concern and whispered, "David, remember where you are."

"Where I am is exactly the problem," said David. "Every year we say, 'Next year in Jerusalem,' but we never do anything about it. We should all go there now, just go! We're the only people on earth without a country."

"Surely there are others, the Gypsies, for instance, or the Armenians?" offered Roger timidly. However, no one took any notice of what he said. They never did.

"Well, I'm not sure we'd fit the terms of the Mandate —" Paul began.

"The Mandate! Forget about the Mandate. England just used the Jews to get Palestine, and now it's selling us out to keep its alliance with the Arabs. Look at the Passfield White Paper, look at the MacDonald White Paper. They've abandoned any pretence of establishing a Jewish homeland."

"Sorry, I'm not as knowledgeable about Zionism as you are, Dovidel," said Bernard, "but I think Britain has been pretty decent about accepting Jewish immigrants to Palestine. Look how many refugees from the Nazis have settled there."

"How few, you ought to say. And anyhow, they've only been admitted over there so they won't come here."

"That's a pretty cynical point of view," Ned remarked. "Is that the general outlook in Oxford?"

"Oxford does not approve of the Hebrew race," David replied in a professorial tone. He placed his palms and fingertips together and glowered over them with furrowed brow and pursed lips.

The twins burst out laughing at this funny face; the others found themselves smiling inadvertently for a moment. Clara hoped that David would be thrown off course and they could resume their meal in peace, but she knew how intransigent he could be. Luckily, their guest seemed to find the argument intriguing rather than disturbing.

David resumed. "Oxford feels that the Hebrew race ought not to appear anywhere but in the Old Testament, and even there, only with the strict understanding that its role is limited to foreshadowing the truths of the Christian Gospel."

"Surely it's not as bad as all that?" Ned aligned his knife and fork across his plate. The food was exceptionally good, as Clara had promised, and the conversation more interesting than he had anticipated.

"Actually, it's worse. I'm sick of all those tweedy Anglicans singing about building Jerusalem in England's green and pleasant land, as though the holy city was just a myth and not a real place where real people lived. Where real people are living right now!"

There was a murmur of assent and a few nods around the table.

"The boy is right," Sidney remarked. "It certainly has a nice tune, but I have to admit that that particular hymn makes me feel uncomfortable too."

But David hadn't finished. Now that he was finally speaking his mind, he wasn't about to be placated. "And I'm sick of reading books where the token Jew is either a crooked banker or a dishonest peddler. If he has a beautiful raven-haired daughter, naturally she has to convert to Christianity so she can run off with the blond hero. And it's not just the classics, it's not just Chaucer and Shakespeare and Dickens, though they're bad enough. But even modern writers repeat the same garbage — T.S. Eliot for example, though I expect none of you are familiar with his work."

"Well, I've always said that literature is not very practical, dear," Alice broke in. "Why don't you give it up and do medicine instead, like Dr. Abraham here? There are lots of Jewish doctors, after all. And everyone knows Jewish doctors are the best."

David made a strangled sound, something between a groan and a snort. As usual, his mother hadn't understood a single word he'd said. But he controlled himself and replied with exaggerated patience. "What I am studying is not the point, Mother. The point is how they really feel about us. Can't you understand? I have to study this stuff, and I find it humiliating. But if I say anything about it, people think I'm over-sensitive. They insist that the characters aren't real Jews, that they're just symbolic. Well, I'm tired of being someone else's symbol. We should all go home, once and for all, and stop pretending we belong."

"Go home? You mean to a tent in a desert?" asked Sidney. Everyone laughed nervously. Their host's joviality was not going to smooth things over so easily. "I doubt you'd be very comfortable there, my boy. England's been good to us. Look around this house. Four bedrooms, two fireplaces, a beautiful garden. And you've had excellent schools, piano lessons, and now Oxford. No one in our family ever went to university before. So what have you lacked?"

"That's obvious — respect! We've all lacked respect, Papa. And I'm sick of trying to fit in all the time. They always know what you are really, and they always find a way to come back at you."

"I agree that there are some ignorant, racially motivated people. God knows we've all had our share of those," said Ned, as the others murmured their assent. "But surely anyone who counts takes one on one's own merit."

"Millie, the girl who does for us, is Irish," offered Clara. "And you would not believe the dreadful things people say about the Irish. It's not only Jews who have problems, David, you must know that. Some people hate anyone who's different from them."

"That just proves my point," David cried.

"Please excuse him, Dr. Abraham, he's young, he gets carried away, he doesn't mean to offend," Sidney offered, deeply embarrassed by his son's behaviour.

"Not at all, Mr. Greenbaum," Ned countered, smiling. "You've no idea how familiar such arguments are to me. After all, my father was an anarchist."

"An anarchist!" Alice exclaimed, as though he'd just said he was an escapee from a leper colony.

"What's a nanarchist?" Evvie inquired.

The children had been remarkably quiet during the adults' discussion. It was quite exciting for them to watch grownups quarrelling — exciting and disturbing as well. They were used to being the troublemakers.

"Someone who believes that ordinary people would do a better job of running things than governments do," Ned replied.

"Then that makes *you* an anarchist, Papa," said Roger, smiling at Sidney. "You're always complaining about the government taxing us to death."

Finally, he had an effect — everyone laughed. Alice, who

had been eyeing Ned rather suspiciously, was momentarily grateful to him for diverting attention away from her wayward son. For his part, Zayde observed the doctor with increased concern: an anarchist and therefore a non-believer, and such an influence on his grandson! He would have to probe him further to see how dangerous he really was.

"Dr. Abraham, would you not say that anarchism is an attack not only on the state but also on religion?" he asked.

Clara was startled; why was her father-in-law pursuing their guest this way? Usually he was the soul of courtesy.

"Yes, certainly. All organized systems of belief are to be questioned according to that philosophy."

"And do you agree with 'that philosophy,' as you call it?"

"Zayde! Enough," Clara interjected. Jacob looked up in alarm. She never talked to his grandfather like that.

"Of course, any thinking person would," burst in David. He was determined not to be diverted from his mission of enlightening his elders. Otherwise they would sit around talking rot and eating too much forever, without questioning the purpose of anything. "Anyhow, the state just uses religion to suppress people, to keep the working man passive in the face of oppression."

Now it was Zayde who intervened, raising his voice for the first time. "To deny people their religion is also a form of oppression, David."

"But you can't have a spiritual life if you're too poor to feed your children," David objected hotly.

"You're wrong, my child," Zayde countered. "I know from experience. The spirit itself feeds you. God is better than bread."

There was a moment's silence before Alice started clucking apologies and compelled David to add a sullen one of his own. The maid was clearing the fish course; Mitzi lumbered back to the table offering to help. Alice waved her away and managed to disengage Edna from her offspring instead to help serve the roast chicken, carrot and prune tsimmes, and potato kugel. The good food absorbed everyone's attention and eased them back into congeniality, though soon the little ones were sleepy and couldn't eat any more. Evvie crawled into her mother's lap, Danny into his grandfather's. Bellies and hearts were full.

Stroking her daughter's shining hair, Clara found herself quietly asking Ned, "How did your mother feel about your father's politics?" Her conscious intention had been to steer the conversation towards something less contentious, but part of her felt compelled to forge on through dangerous territory. This man had begun to interest her more and more, in an unfamiliar way. In her family everyone ate too much too quickly, everyone talked too loudly. But there was an alluring refinement about Dr. Abraham. His voice was so tranquil, his long-fingered hands so elegant, his black eyes so unfathomable. Unlike Uncle Sidney, who had second helpings of everything, he left half the food uneaten on his plate, and such restraint was tantalizing. Their guest seemed to be having the same effect on the other women at the table, for even Mitzi, mute behind the mountain of her belly, couldn't stop staring at him, and Alice kept fussing with her coiffure and adjusting her dress for maximum effect.

"My mother? Well, to be honest, I've never been sure what she believes. She certainly grew up religious. Her father had been the shammes, you know, the caretaker of his little shul, and he also taught the local children Hebrew."

"Ah!" cried Zayde, who was listening intently though the conversation was meant to be private. "I thought so. You come from a good family, I could tell."

Ned laughed ruefully. His mother's chief vanity had always been that she was educated while most of the other mothers in the Leylands were not.

"Anyhow, one day, they took all the boys of the village away, including her brother Eli. I'm named after him."

"The Russian army did that all the time," Zayde nodded. "Many boys in our village too, young, some only ten or eleven like my Yakov here, skinny, in rags even in winter. They made them march and march to death. Or they made them eat trayf and baptized them so that even if they survived, they were too ashamed to return to their families."

"Did you know anyone like that, Zayde?" Jacob asked, startled. No one had told him these stories before.

"Yes, many. Those were terrible times, but never again, halevai."

"Maybe that's what happened to my uncle," Ned remarked. "He never came home."

"And your mother?" Clara continued.

"My mother missed him a lot. It was a terrible time for her family. Shortly after Eli went away there was a pogrom and her father died, running into the burning shul to rescue the holy books."

Mutterings and sighs around the table. A tear rolled down Clara's face. Evvie started to whimper in sympathy.

"What did your mother, I mean your grandmother, do then?" asked Alice.

"Well, eventually it got too hard in the village. They couldn't really make a living selling eggs and whatnot, so they moved to town, where my mother went into service to a rich family. And then she married my father and had a baby. They all lived together in two rooms, and when the old lady got scarlet fever so did the baby, and one of my mother's younger sisters too. Only the sister survived. When my mother found herself pregnant again, they decided to immigrate to England. My older sister was born just before they left, but I was born here."

"And coming from all that, your mother let you grow up without Torah?" Zayde said quietly.

"Coming from all that, she lost her faith, yes."

"But you've come to us for Pesach," said Sidney. "So let us be hopeful that one day you may find it in your heart to forgive the Almighty, who forgives all of us. And meanwhile, let's have another glass of wine and finish our service. There's still an afikohmen to find and money for the children who find it. Who wants to open the door for Elijah this year?"

"Me, me!" all the children shouted at once. The twins were already out of their chairs, pushing each other out of the way. Edna got up and took them each by a hand, whispering that they would go together to look for the hidden matzo.

"Did I ever tell you about the time back in Russia when my Zayde opened the door and a goat walked in?" he continued.

"Yes, Uncle Sidney, you tell us every year," Jacob laughed, relieved at the restoration of predictability. "But tell us again. Tell us again."

After the Seder was over, Alice waved Clara away, she had plenty of help, why didn't Clara show their guest the grounds? They were as grand as the house and equally formal. Neither Alice nor Sidney ever worked outdoors, but they were very proud of the effect achieved by their well-paid gardener and liked to show it off.

Glad of an excuse to get away from the overtired and increasingly rowdy children, Ned offered Clara his arm and they strolled out. A half-moon glinted hazily behind a halo of white; it would rain tomorrow. The breeze was already damp, and Clara shivered, pulling her paisley shawl closer. There was a slight rip at one corner; she twisted her finger round and round in it, thinking, I must mend that, why didn't I mend that before I came? He must think I am so dowdy compared to the other women he knows. And he must know so many other women.

They did a cursory round of the garden, Ned blowing contemplative smoke-rings, Clara stopping from time to time to deadhead a spent blossom. Aromatic yellow roses bloomed around a pseudo-Roman fountain which, in its turn, emptied into a pond full of fat red and silver mottled carp. Ned flicked his ash at the surface, and the fish rose at once to his fraudulent bait. Beyond the pond was a gazebo draped with wisteria. It looked like a stage set.

"I apologize for my family. Sometimes I forget how loud and intrusive they can be."

She paused, and he murmured politely, "Not at all, not at all."

"I'm used to it." She laughed, surprised at the bitterness in her voice. "One learns to talk as a form of self-defence really, to hide rather than reveal what one is thinking. Because if you are too quiet, everyone's always bothering you."

"I know exactly what you mean," he replied. He met her eyes, so green and lucid.

"Still, I suppose you're rarely confronted like *that*."

"More often than you might think. My practice is in Hackney, so most of my patients are Jewish. For some reason I seem to attract a lot of old ladies, and sometimes they treat me like a son. Or worse, a prospective son-in-law."

"How can you bear it?" He seemed so austere, not one to tolerate undue familiarity.

"I just shut them out. Being a doctor is useful that way. It's easy to change the topic, write a prescription, take a pulse, and assert your authority. You put on quite a bit of authority with that white coat."

"Is that why you went into medicine?"

"One of the reasons."

"But you're such a wonderful musician. Didn't you ever consider pursuing violin professionally?"

Although this was a question people often asked him, each time it stabbed. His inadequacy was a splinter that could not be removed; though it was callused over, he could still feel it embedded there. But over the years, he'd evolved a stock answer that made him sound content. So he offered it to Clara, wondering if it would satisfy her.

"Well, let's just say I prefer to keep music a private pleasure. Amateurs don't have to please anyone but themselves. Because I don't play for money, it's pure. It's an escape from work, if you like. An escape to a better world."

"A better world," repeated Clara. "How I wish I could go there."

So she hadn't been judging him after all, just making conversation. Ned relaxed, watching the fish circle, circle, going nowhere. In the silvery dusk, it felt as though he too were suspended under water.

"Which comes first, I wonder, music or words?" Clara asked after a moment or two. The moon in the sky and the moon in the pond both wavered, indistinct, reflections of each other.

"Music, surely," Ned replied with passion. "My teacher Gustave Rose calls it drumming and humming."

"Drumming and humming. What a lovely phrase! I've never heard that before. I suppose it means that music is instinctive?"

"Yes. The rest is all chatter, compromise, blah blah blah. We just get further and further away from what we mean the more we talk. But music is different. It *is* what it says. It's complete in itself. Untranslatable."

"Do you really think so?"

"Absolutely. What music expresses is eternal, ideal. Not the daily nonsense about shoes and soup, but what matters. Not you or me in our littleness, but in our universality."

"But if we become universal, don't we lose who we really are?"

"Not at all. We reveal what is deepest in us, our hidden desires. The truths of our inner nature. Music speaks to that directly. Words just separate people and make them miserable. But music brings them together."

What a strange man he was, to be so excited by ideas. To scorn what everyone else loved: carrot coins gleaming in broth, the blunt faces of shoes. This must be why she was so drawn to him. They both knew there had to be more to life than the surface of things, their endless replication and maintenance.

The fragrance of roses was everywhere, diffused in the misty air. She was getting dizzy from inhaling it, from the unexpected intensity of the conversation, or perhaps only from Ned's physical proximity. Why did standing next to him make Clara feel that her real life had passed her by? She'd never met anyone quite like him before: a man whose passionate gaze met hers so directly while giving nothing away; a man whose every word was at once an invitation to intimacy and a polite withdrawal from it. Of course, she'd never known any man at all except poor Leonard. She prayed Ned couldn't tell she was blushing. It was absurd to be so aroused by a virtual stranger.

Then somehow, he had thrown away his cigarette, taken her hand, and pulled her with him into the gazebo. They were well screened from the brightly lit windows of the house, through which they could hear, as though from miles away, the yelps of children chasing around the living room. And then he was kissing her, very gently.

Was it just kindness? Or did he want her as she wanted him?

His lips were so soft, as soft as a child's. Without thinking, Clara kissed him back. Then she nestled into him, her whole self pushing forward, insistent, against his chest, till he put his arms around her. They fit together very well, her face upturned to his at chin level. Briefly, she thought of Magda Tabori, so much taller, wondering if he was in love with her. It had seemed so at the concert, but there was so much about him she didn't know. But now she knew a little more, for their skins had spoken to each other. His was pleasantly abrasive, like a cat's tongue, with a slightly sharp tang: black liquorice, ginger-root, tea steeped too long in the pot. And when he kissed her, she was as shocked by her own lack of hesitation as by the knowing familiarity in his embrace.

They must stop now, they absolutely must. Someone might see them, one of the children perhaps.

But she didn't want to stop. There was something irrevocable about the moment, even though it was quite absurd. The gazebo, the fountain, and the roses made such a hackneyed recipe for romance. She observed herself kissing this stranger as if she were a character in some shoddy novel and still felt the strongest physical desire she'd ever experienced. How could this be?

She heard herself say, "We must go back in." Her voice sounded blessedly firm.

And she heard him answer, "Of course," and "Sorry, I got a little carried away. I do apologize."

And then she didn't know what to say anymore, and they walked back in silence as the last colours drained from the garden and clouds blanketed the moon and it grew suddenly much colder. And, after all, it was time to go home.

The Inner Ear

Music is the art of time, pure temporality abstracted from word or concept. Time as experienced by God and only guessed at by man — rhythm and cadence, variable and pliant as air. Music is what you hear whenever you really listen. It can be as rapid as an infant's heartbeat or as slow as the earth's crust wearing away. And music is the art that stops time. Playing music, you are too far inside time to measure it; caught in the vortices of sound, you cannot fathom whether one hour has passed or two. You are only playing towards, not from — towards the unattainable, the ideal performance. And after that performance what else can there be but silence? Music is the art that seeks its own extinction.

Or so Ned told Jacob, who listened, spellbound if a little lost. He too wished to stop time, to live beyond its reach where the people he loved could never be taken away. If he could play his mother, his sister, brother, and grandfather, he would never let them go.

But Ned said no, that was sentimental and not what he meant. Feelings about people would have to be left outside too, otherwise we would have only the most vulgar kind of programme music. What was required was pure essence, pure abstraction.

"You mean songs without words?"

"Exactly."

Maybe that was what Mendelssohn had been after, Jacob thought. So *he* could stop talking, talking to himself as well as to others. So he could silence all the voices. Silence the kids at school who called him a Christ-killer and made fun of his clumsiness at sports. Stop trying to explain what could never be explained: why he found refuge in the piano, why he had no father, why his granddad wore such funny clothes and spoke with such a funny accent.

So many things separated people and made them miserable and suspicious and confused. Maybe if they all just stopped talking for a while, when they returned to language they'd have to find a new one, one they could invent together.

Jacob invited Dr. Abraham to his house for a final practice the last Sunday before the concert. Aunt Alice took Evvie and Danny to Kew Gardens for a treat so the musicians could perform undisturbed. Clara made her special sticky plum cake and put out the best china.

"Charming house you have, Mrs. Weiss," said Ned.

Not really. The place was terribly cluttered and none of the furniture matched. The colours were nice, however, warm and inviting golds and greens that set off Clara's hair. There were even some decent paintings on the wall: two Impressionist-style landscapes and a Dutch-looking bowl of fruit, with a glistening water drop rolling down the side of one plump peach. Ned rocked on his heels for a moment, considering the water drop through half-closed eyes. Just a flake of white pigment up close, but a spangle of light, a glitter of crystal, from farther away. An optical trick or a comment on the nature of reality?

"Thank you. We are happy here," Clara replied, in a silly tea-party voice. Not her voice at all.

Why was he studying that picture so intently? Had he noticed her signature on it? He must be as embarrassed as she was. How could she have hung it on the wall like that, as though she were a real painter?

"Would you like a cup of tea before you begin? You must be thirsty after coming all this way." The garden — she dare not invite him into the garden, not with Jacob here. She did not trust herself.

"Tea would be splendid." He pulled up a chair. "And how are you today, Jacob?"

"Fine, thank you, Dr. Abraham. It's strange to see you here at my house, but it was really nice of you to come."

The boy was so excited he could barely sit still. Clara quietly reminded him not to fidget. It saddened her seeing him like this, for it made her realize how few visitors they had and how few special occasions were just for him. Evvie and Danny were always quarrelling and making a mess. She was always rushing around fixing things, trying to make them happy. It was nice for Jacob to be the centre of attention for once.

"Have you lived here long?" Ned asked. He estimated that tea would take ten or fifteen minutes, the music perhaps forty-five, and then he could leave, claiming business across town. An hour of other people's lives was about his limit, the length of a thorough medical examination.

"Always. I mean, since we got married, Leonard and I. When we bought the house it was still on gas. We put in the electricity and the telephone. But it was in decent shape otherwise, nothing we couldn't manage."

"Papa was good at fixing things," offered Jacob. His happiest memories of his father were of them playing workmen together. He even had a miniature tool kit with a shiny hammer, a screwdriver, and pliers that really worked. It was time to pass them on to Danny, but Jacob didn't feel ready yet. His little brother would probably break the tools or lose them.

"That must be where you got your eye-hand coordination, Jacob," Ned was saying, pleased with himself for thinking of this remark. It had the right tone: kind, avuncular, yet detached.

The boy smiled and added loyally, "But my mother plays piano too, you know, and she paints. She painted all these pictures."

"Really?" Ned remarked, standing up to study the still life again. "These are excellent, Mrs. Weiss. I didn't know you were as talented as Jacob."

"Thank you, Dr. Abraham. It's just a hobby."

She was very embarrassed. She had wanted so badly for him to admire her, but now she felt silly and pretentious.

Noticing her discomfort, Ned changed the subject. "Was your father artistic too, Jacob?"

"Papa? No, not really. Was he, Mum?"

"It depends what you mean by artistic. Everything he did, he did well, very neatly and precisely, with good concentration. But he'd never had an opportunity to do any kind of art or music because he'd worked ever since he was a boy. His mother died when he was very young, you see, and he and his father lived alone, over the shop."

"What kind of shop?" Ned inquired politely. What did he

care what kind of shop? Under the table his knee jigged up and down impatiently.

"A drapery. We still have it, Jacob's grandfather and I, in Whitechapel."

"Would you tell me more about your father, please?" asked Jacob. "Was he a doctor like you? What did he do? I mean, besides being an anarchist."

"Most of the time he worked in a factory, cutting cloth for clothes. Until no one would employ him anymore because he made too much trouble."

"What kind of trouble? Did he break things?"

"No, nothing like that. But he was always trying to organize the workers and then, when he got them into a union, he would try to get the union to challenge the government."

"How do you do that?"

"Well, you remember your cousin David, at the Seder, arguing with everybody about Israel? He reminded me of my father. That's what my father did too, he was always arguing with people. Not because he was angry with them, just because he had strong opinions. He also organized protests, wrote articles, and made speeches. He tried to make people think."

"And what about your mother?" Jacob was suddenly aware of his own, smiling intently at him, delighted that he was having this adult conversation. He didn't often see her this happy.

"My mother just kept quiet and kept working. Luckily Sir Montague Burton, her employer, didn't care about Papa's reputation."

"It must have been so hard for her," Clara observed. "To have to leave her children and go to work every day."

"Actually, I don't think it was, not for my mother anyway. She enjoyed her work and she liked to keep busy. To be honest, she's never been very domestic. I think having to clean other people's houses for a living when she was young cured her of domesticity forever."

"But what did she do with you?" she asked.

"Oh, I stayed with the neighbours. First one, then another. And when I was older obviously there was school, and my sister Alta looked after me."

"Were they nice?" Jacob asked.

"Who?"

"The neighbours."

Ned had to laugh at that. How intense they were, this family. They talked as though all this had happened only yesterday.

"One was, the first one, but she moved away. Too many kids for the flat. But it was fun for me because there were so many people to play with. The second lady wasn't as nice. I don't think she really liked me, and she had no children of her own. She took in laundry and spent the whole day scrubbing and hanging out and ironing, and I had to keep out of the way and be quiet. But she had a cat, a fluffy grey cat, with odd eyes: one blue and one green. Mostly I played with him. Actually, I don't remember much about those days. I had forgotten all about that cat until you reminded me. I can't even remember his name. Pierrot? Harlequin? Something like that, I think. A bit pretentious, really, for a grubby little mouser. Maybe that lady had wanted to be an actress or something, and that's why she was so bad-tempered. Everyone in the Leylands dreamed of a better life."

"What's the Leylands?" asked Jacob.

"The poor part of Leeds I grew up in. A lot of Jewish immigrants lived there. Most of them, like my parents, came from Russia. And many people wished they'd go back."

"What do you mean?"

"Well, when the war started, there was rioting in the streets of Leeds against the Jews. After running away from pogroms in the first place, they weren't too keen on fighting to save the dear old Tsar. So they were declared traitors to England. But since the immigration department wouldn't allow them to become soldiers, they couldn't have fought even if they'd wanted to . . . oh, the whole thing was absurd, really."

"Dr. Abraham, you keep saying *they*," Jacob remarked.

"They what?"

"You keep calling Jewish people *they*, not *we*."

"Well, to be honest, that's how it's always felt."

Ned paused, unwilling to discuss his religious convictions — or lack of them — with this child. Especially in front of Clara, who was looking at him with the face of a Botticelli madonna. Taking him in as a lost sheep, as one of the tribe, when he felt as distant as ever from the whole notion of a tribe. More than distant, really: in active opposition to such a notion. Families were always so exhausting. He had made a terrible mistake getting involved with one again.

So he changed the topic.

"I have to say, my father and his mates did their best to annoy people, marching around with big signs saying things like, 'Turn Your Guns on your Real Enemies! Down with Bloodthirsty Capitalism' and 'Refuse to Fire on your German Brothers! Unite for Peace!' He even got thrown in jail once for public rioting."

"Really? Your father went to jail?" Jacob was incredulous. Fathers didn't go to jail. Fathers fixed things and bought things and took you to shul and made you do your lessons. Every morning they shaved and went off to work; every night they read you a story and tucked you into bed. Fathers were reliable. Unless, of course, they died.

"At least he wasn't pretending how brave and fine it was to go off and be killed for your country," Clara interjected. "That's what happened to my brother Jacob. He was only nineteen years old when he died, but he wanted so much to be a hero. It didn't occur to my family to question whether that war was worth fighting in the first place."

And then Clara was crying, actually crying. He'd been selfish, as usual, assuming that her only interest was in what he had to say. Of course she had her own stories too. Ned turned to the boy, embarrassed.

"Aha, your uncle was named Jacob. Then you must be named after him, as I'm named after my Uncle Eli."

"Yes, that's right," Jacob replied eagerly. His attention was firmly fixed on Ned, his new idol. He hadn't even noticed his mother dabbing away at her tears with a napkin.

"Well then, we have a lot in common, don't we? Including Mozart. So why don't we play?"

And he led the boy to the piano, leaving Clara to collect herself. Surely she would prefer to be alone.

Clara busied herself with the tea things. She didn't know whether she was more humiliated at bursting into tears or angry with Ned and Jacob for ignoring her. She felt as if she was losing her son to this man, this stranger, so haughty and self-important. So good at keeping his distance, always in control.

If she could only forget that kiss in the garden.

She dreamed of it nightly. The weather was becoming warm, and under her thin nightgown her body turned, seeking his shadow in her bed. She stroked her own breasts, feeling the nipples harden, then her belly, and down and down. But the hands drawing music from her were his hands. She imagined exactly how they would feel.

And here he was, in his soft grey suit, gold cufflinks, silk tie: self-contained, distant, not even looking at her. As though the body she had imagined so vividly wasn't right there, under the fine attire. As though he were cool silk, not warm flesh, all the way through. And she in a foolish ruffled apron like someone in a shop: cheap, ignorant, beneath his notice. Shame suffused her, right to the roots of her hair, red, red, burning. She couldn't breathe.

"Yes, you two go ahead and have a good practice now. I must see to something in the kitchen." She almost ran from the room.

The ear collects sound as a flower does dew, channels it along the auditory canal to brew a secret honey. The air flutters, the air is alive with wings; sound waves drum against the ear and set its architecture humming. Sensation is transformed into energy like dew into nectar. And then (but this is no explanation, this is just the map of a mystery) the mind gives meaning to what it hears.

The concert was a big success. This time Alice came, and Sidney, and even cousin Paul. Since the Seder, they'd become intrigued by Dr. Abraham and wanted to see him and Jacob play together. Two fine dark profiles, two small slender bodies, two sets of nimble fingers. The pair could have been father and son — as everyone told Clara, much to her chagrin.

The Mozart was note-perfect, though not as incandescent as it had been in those practice sessions with Miss Westerham. Somehow the intensity of her regard had pushed the musicians to the limit of expression; the shuffling, whispering audience in the Guildhall didn't seem to demand the same refinement of them. And their own nerves failed to carry them there. So Ned and Jacob were rather disappointed, despite the enthusiastic response.

"You two should go on tour together!" Uncle Sidney pumped Ned's hand and patted Jacob on the back, puffing with pride and cigar-smoke. "I'll be your backer, what do you say? The Continent, America, wherever you want to go. We'll make a fortune."

Aunt Alice was no less exuberant, telling anyone who would listen that her nephew, Jacob, that little boy over there, was not yet twelve years old, and asking if they'd ever heard anyone more talented in their lives. Her poor sister was raising three children all by herself, you really had to give her credit. Of course, she herself helped out from time to time and was happy to think that she might have had some influence on the boy, though God knows she had no musical talent whatsoever, none whatsoever, as anyone might appreciate who'd had the misfortune to hear her sing. Cousin Paul just stood there quietly, a big smile on his affable, homely face.

Only Clara was as restrained as the musicians themselves, sharing a little of their letdown. She too felt that something was missing in the concert hall that had been present in the studio; a certain intelligence of interpretation had been supplanted by showy banality. Until now, Ned and Jacob had always played to each other, not to the crowd. But their attention had been diluted by the occasion. Or maybe it was that they needed Miss Westerham as a kind of compass. Her passion, greater, in its way, than theirs, had kept them focused.

But if Miss Westerham herself was disappointed, she didn't show it. Resplendent in yellow silk, with several strands of enormous coral beads looped around her neck, she listened to Alice with great good humour, returned Sidney's hearty handshake, and even managed to coax a few words out of bashful cousin Paul. Then she turned to Magda, whom she could detect approaching in a fragrant cloud of Arpège. After sneezing reproachfully, she asked, "Well, Madame Tabori, what do you think? Wasn't I right about those two working well together?"

"It was a stroke of genius, dear Miss Westerham," Magda replied, giving the older woman an affectionate kiss on one wrinkled, rouged cheek. "And I think it sets a wonderful example for the rest of the school, pairing an experienced musician with a young student. We should do it more often."

"But I don't know how many of the adults here would be as generous as Dr. Abraham with their time. What do you think, Ned?"

"I really couldn't say. I didn't find it too difficult, but that may be because Jacob is such a pleasure to be with."

He had his arm around the boy, who was grinning, too happy even to explore the refreshment table. If only he could stay like this forever, Dr. Abraham hugging him while his mother stood by, smiling fondly. Jacob was in heaven.

Moved by the boy's delight, Magda was nonetheless aware of a prickle of sexual tension between the two adults who stood on either side of him, avoiding each others' eyes. Now *that* was interesting. Surely Ned wasn't going to pursue someone as obviously susceptible as Jacob's mother? Probably he couldn't help himself, men were hopeless that way. Magda's experience inclined her to expect little restraint from the opposite sex, but she doubted whether young widow Weiss had much knowledge in that regard. Would raising three children by herself have given her the skills to manage someone as skittish as Ned?

Magda regarded the pair coolly, trying to decide if it would work. Clara, becoming aware of the singer's scrutiny, wondered whether her new dress had, after all, been a mistake. Or was it the hat? Silly really, that green feather, it made her look like Robin Hood. She'd never measure up to someone like Magda, but at least this time she'd made an effort to be stylish. Probably Ned hadn't noticed anyway; he'd barely said a word to her all night. Luckily, everyone was leaving, so she need not waste any more time trying to impress him.

But as she was saying her goodbyes, he came over to her with a friendly smile. "Mrs. Weiss, I wonder if I might invite you and Jacob out for an ice cream?"

"Isn't it awfully late?"

"Please Mum? Please? There's no school tomorrow, and I didn't get a chance to eat anything here. I'm starving!" begged Jacob, determined to make this night last as long as possible.

"Oh, all right," she replied, laughing. "Just this once. But don't forget Millie needs to leave at a reasonable hour. I'd better ring her and say we'll be a little longer than expected."

"Thank you, thank you! What's your favourite flavour, Dr. Abraham? Mine's chocolate."

"Then I guess I'll have to have chocolate too."

They walked down John Carpenter Street to the Embankment where, if they were lucky, there might be an ice cream cart at this late hour. People strolled about, enjoying the balmy May evening, and, sure enough, many of them brandished ice cream cones. Ned insisted on buying Jacob two scoops even though Clara protested, and as they ate they leaned over the water, admiring the river traffic against the sunset sky. Ned recited:

> *Earth has not anything to show more fair:*
> *Dull would he be of soul who could pass by*
> *A sight so touching in its majesty.*

"Wordsworth?" asked Clara.

"Yes, the sonnet on Westminster Bridge, one of my favourite poems."

"It's odd though, isn't it? I mean, we all think of Wordsworth as the poet of nature. But then he says that this city is the fairest thing on earth."

"Well, not quite. He says the fairest thing is this city when it's sound asleep in the early morning," Ned replied, smiling, "before the business day begins, when London is at one with nature instead of separate from it."

"We had to do that poem at school," Jacob broke in, eager to be included.

"So do you like it?"

"It's not too bad. At least I understand what he's saying, which is better than most of the rubbish we have to read."

"What's your favourite subject, then?" asked Ned.

"I don't know. Maths, I guess."

"That was always mine as well."

Ned lost interest in his ice cream cone and threw it to a crippled pigeon with a single twisted pink foot. The bird took a couple of excited pecks before an enormous seagull swooped down out of nowhere and flew off with the prize.

"Well, *that's* the true face of nature in London!" he remarked.

"The nerve of those gulls," Clara said. "Here, my sweet. Come here, little one, and you can have mine instead." She crouched, clucking softly at the one-legged bird that eventually, warily, hopped over and took the food from her hand.

"Mum, he's so tame," Jacob said.

"He would have to be, wouldn't he, to survive around here? He can't compete with the other pigeons by fighting, so if he weren't a good beggar, he'd be dead."

"But you never see any dead pigeons anywhere. Where do they all go?"

"The street sweepers probably pick them up in the morning. That's when they clean up the bodies in the river too," said Ned.

"Are there lots of them? Bodies in the river, I mean?"

"They say there's at least one a week. But I've only seen one myself, quite recently," Ned replied. "Just last autumn."

"Who was it?" Clara's arms went around Jacob as if to protect him from what they were hearing.

"I have no idea. A man with a long grey beard, that's all I know. I couldn't find anything about it in the papers, though I looked for weeks. I still wonder who he was and how he came to be in the river. For a long time I kept dreaming about him. It was strange."

"How awful!"

"Actually, it's not the worst way to die. They say drowning's rather peaceful. Our bodies are ninety-five per cent water anyway, so there's always a pull to return to the first element. Look at us, we were drawn right to the river."

"Surely wanting to look at the water isn't the same as deciding to jump in and drown."

"No, of course not. I'm sorry if I upset you, Mrs. Weiss. It was tactless of me to bring this up, really."

"Oh well, don't mind me," Clara said. Once again she had overreacted. He must think her a fool by now. "I'm just tired. I'm sure we all are after such an exciting evening. Jacob, if you're finally finished eating, let's go home. It really is late now."

"I didn't come by car tonight, unfortunately, or I'd offer you a lift. But I'll walk you to the tube, shall I?"

"Thank you, Dr. Abraham, that would be nice. Come *on*, Jacob."

Ned watched them go down the stairs to the underground arm in arm, so comfortable together. By the time he was Jacob's age his mother would never have held his hand in public. Not that she'd ever done it much even when he was small, except to steer him safely across a busy street. But Jacob was much less inhibited physically than Ned had been at that age. Probably that was a good thing; it was hard to say. Maybe it would get him into trouble one day, being too demonstrative.

He would love meeting Jacob ten years down the road to see how he'd turned out. Would he go into his rich uncle's fur business and become another vaguely dissatisfied businessman, eating too much, working too hard, and playing the piano only on special occasions? Would he succumb to the ennui of the parlour, taking refuge in his newspaper from the prattling of his wife? Or would that darkness in him, that intensity which spoke to the same darkness in Ned, carry him abroad to the cafés and studios of Europe, to the goyim and their unattainable women?

Magda had definitely been right to suggest a similarity between them. Ned felt more than affection for this lonely, brilliant child; he felt responsibility for him in a way he scarcely understood. Maybe this was what fathers felt for their children — proper fathers, that is, unlike his own, who'd run away. Still, he reminded himself that his encouragement could do no more than reinforce a drive, a passion, that was Jacob's own, and one that others had recognized and cultivated before him. Miss Westerham obviously, but also his mother, Clara, despite her constant air of distraction.

Clara. Clara. What should he do about *her*?

It was tempting to pursue her invitation, so openly given, so urgent. He could tell she would be good in bed; her body had a certain confidence, the way it insinuated its shape into his arms. And after all she was a widow, so this time there would be no irate husband to avoid. But that was exactly why the thing was too risky. She was free, and freedom was something he reserved for himself.

Anyhow, she wasn't really his type, though pretty enough in a hazy, pre-Raphaelite way. But dowdy. Too much hair, too much flesh, not enough makeup. And provincial, really, obsessed by her children and her garden. No accomplishments. Although when he thought about it, her painting was actually quite good.

And then he remembered the absolute unclouded intelligence in her green eyes, the candour of that gaze, and knew there was more to her than maternal preoccupation. Maybe she didn't pay attention all the time because most things didn't merit her full regard. After all, she was dealing with trivia most days, not with the kind of problems he dealt with, scientific problems that might have genuine solutions. He'd never actually thought about this before, he'd only known that domesticity repelled him. Like the tumult at his sister's house, the constant pacification of whining children at the seder and the rushing about with food and drink had reminded him of everything he disliked, and why.

He reckoned women like Clara must operate differently from men. How else could they bear having to do two or three things at a time, always leaving things half-done, always being interrupted? A civilized person needed to be able to pursue a line of thought uninterrupted. He would be miserable in the world Clara inhabited; he was convinced of that.

Clara boarded the underground at Hammersmith determined, in spite of herself, to enjoy the ride. Each stop might reveal something new: society ladies at South Kensington and Sloan Square, travellers burdened by maps and suitcases at Victoria, bowler-hatted men at St. James. She was always amused by the juxtaposition of Temple and Blackfriars, so much like her own little neighbourhood with the synagogue on one side of Brook Green and Holy Trinity Church on the other. Even underground, London was a city of contrast and of constant adventure.

Nevertheless, she came up at Aldgate East with her usual sigh of relief and shook herself like a terrier coming out of the water. She liked to see where she was going, whereas the underground might be anywhere dark and unlovely, dank and smelly. A cave. A cage. It was all wrong somehow, though one had to use it these days to get across London in reasonable time. So much traffic everywhere, everyone in a mad rush.

And indeed Whitechapel High Street, though always busy, seemed unusually full of people — hot, dirty people running, shoving, and shouting. What a stench! Didn't they wash? What on earth was going on? There was such a throng. She would have to ask Zayde. Every Monday she had lunch with him at the shop and they did the accounts together; it was the least she could do in exchange for the income the business provided. Then, on Friday, Zayde came to them for Shabbes. So his week was bookended by family, and she didn't have to feel guilty about him living by himself.

Clara turned up Commercial and then left again at Wentworth. The workday jumble of colours and sounds never failed to delight her. Markets made the world seem so full of possibilities because, for once, everything you could think of was right within reach. Shiny black suits swayed from their racks like men praying before a table full of chipped and mismatched crockery. A grey-bearded bookseller stood engrossed in his own wares, oblivious to the tumult around him, while costermongers in flowered pinafores raised equally bright voices in competition for the attention of passersby. Fat babies in pushchairs gnawed at bagels while their mothers bargained over chickens swinging upside down like bizarre chandeliers from the butcher's negligent hands. Although her mother had always bought fowl live and plucked them at home, Clara couldn't bear to do it herself. But her weekly trip to the market always made her feel that life was going on as it should, that it would continue forever in the same comfortable patterns of buying and selling and cleaning and cooking, generation after generation.

However, at the next corner the atmosphere suddenly changed. The first thing Clara noticed was a glittering pile of broken glass in the street. What a shame, a broken shop window. Or no, it looked like two shops had suffered damage. With a growing sense of dread, she walked over to a woman who leaned on her broom, weeping. Yes, the shopkeeper replied, yes, it had been Owen Burke and that lot, Oswald Mosley's thugs: the Blackshirts. They were determined to take the East End by terror. And they'd started up a new tactic: open-air rallies at night, vans driving through Jewish neighbourhoods with loudspeakers shouting anti-Semitic propaganda just when people were trying to settle their children to sleep. Windows had to be open against the heat in those overcrowded flats, so no one could escape the verbal assault. But if they shouted back, the Blackshirts took it as provocation and started smashing things.

Clara had heard rumours about this kind of violence but hadn't realized the extent of it. She'd put it down to a few unemployed hooligans despite the fact that the British Union of Fascists was a big organization and had a lot of followers. Why did she persist in closing her eyes and hugging her children to her, hoping numbly for the best? She read the papers. She listened to the radio. She knew there was darkness in the world.

Her heart started to pound worse than it had on the underground, and she ran faster down the street, lifting her skirt, jumping over rubble, weaving in and out of the muttering crowd.

Suddenly, a voice called her name; she looked up from

the littered pavement. At the corner of Bell Lane, she saw Zayde standing outside his shop, pointing at something. The front window had been spared, thank God, but something was painted on the wall, something bright red, dripping like blood. "P.J."

"What is it, Zayde?" she shouted. "What does it mean?"

"Perish Judea."

She ran to the man who was almost her father, over bricks and broken glass, wildly. And fell.

Zayde stumbled to her and helped her up. It hurt. Her shin was bleeding profusely, red like the letters on the wall. Something stabbed, sharp and deep; darkness swirled around her and she had to sit down again, her head between her knees. Her face was wet too. More blood? No, just tears.

"I'm all right, thank you, Zayde. Just a little dizzy," she replied to the old man's worried inquiries. She lifted her dirty skirt and stared at the gash on her leg.

"Actually, that looks rather messy," said an unexpected but familiar voice.

She looked up.

"Dr. Abraham! What on earth are *you* doing here?"

She was mortified to be found sitting in the dirt, her skirt hiked up and her shin all bloody. But he seemed quite calm, immediately kneeling down to examine the wound through her torn stocking.

"I was seeing a house-bound patient, just over the way," he replied, "one of those old ladies I told you about. She's getting over pneumonia and is too weak to make it to my office, so I just popped in to check on her. The disturbances here last night didn't do her any good, unfortunately. How about you, Mr. Weiss? How are you holding up?"

"Me? I'm fine, thank God," Zayde replied. "But my dear Clara — so much blood. Is it bad?"

Clara gasped at Ned's probing fingers, nearly fainting again.

"It's not serious, just messy." He brushed off his knees and helped Clara to her feet, keeping a steady grip on her forearm so she wouldn't fall again. His manner was entirely professional. Either he hadn't noticed that she was trembling when he touched her or he just put it down to the shock and pain of the accident.

"Look," he continued, "there is definitely some glass in there. You ought to have it cleaned out right away, and then you'll need some stitches, I'm afraid. I've got a car. Where would you like me to take you? I don't recommend the hospital, they'll keep you waiting for ages. Who's your doctor?"

"Dr. Salansky. He's in the West End," Clara started to say, just as Zayde broke in, "Can't you fix it yourself, Dr. Abraham?"

"If you like," Ned replied. "I was on my way back to the surgery anyway. My car's right down the street. Can you manage to walk that far?"

"It's just a cut. Honestly, I'll be fine," said Clara. She was getting more and more flustered as the bleeding continued, soaking through the handkerchief Ned had knotted around her leg. Her head was spinning. Couldn't someone else just make a decision and take care of *her* for once?

"Go, shayne, please," said Zayde.

"Come along then," said Ned, recognizing her confusion. And as he took her by one arm and her father-in-law by the other to the nice shiny automobile smelling of warm leather and tobacco, and they settled her in the back with her leg propped up, she realized that someone else was taking care of her after all.

Ned was good at taking care of people, Clara could see that. His manner was so smooth that it freed her from all embarrassment. Nonetheless, she shuddered each time he touched her, and he touched her often — helping her out of the car into his clean white office, swabbing her leg, probing it gently as the glass of brandy he gave her started to work. She was ashamed of herself; his behaviour was entirely proper. He had never alluded to that single foolish moment in Alice's garden and never would. It had meant nothing to him. Of course not! He liked glamorous women like Magda Tabori. Why on earth would he want her?

But even though her injured leg was numb now, the rest of her burned. It wasn't the brandy, it was his presence suffusing her body. She watched him stitch up the ugly gash, the pain distant, thrumming away in the background like an old wound remembered. She noticed that the black thread he used was about the same colour and thickness as the hair on the backs of his hands, and she felt an overpowering urge to catch and hold one of those hands, long-fingered, graceful, absolutely impersonal as they went about their work.

Or were they? Had he just stroked her leg? Gently, it was true, but still, unprofessionally? Surely that was a caress, surely he too was breathing a little faster than before? Weren't his hands moving higher than absolutely required for dressing her wound? Dressing, undressing; would he? Would they?

The rustling of leaves is rated at ten decibels, a whisper at twenty, an ordinary conversation at sixty-five, a moving train at one hundred. Any sound over one hundred and twenty decibels is experienced as pain, not sound. Too much of anything, even beauty, is experienced as pain. Think about that.

The decibel is one tenth of the bel, a measurement of amplitude named in honour of Alexander Graham Bell, who also invented the telephone, perfected the phonograph, and taught the deaf. Like Beethoven, only in reverse. Beethoven wrote music he couldn't hear for the pleasure of others. Bell, who could hear, made a language for those who couldn't. Translating sounds to signs, or electrical impulses, in the ear or along a wire, into voices, into music. Vibration, simple vibration, is what makes all bodies resound. And at the lowest register, sound waves are felt on the skin, the body itself resonating like a drum.

He could translate what her body was saying. He knew it was saying yes. But her voice was so soft he could barely hear it, a whisper, twenty decibels at most. Or maybe she hadn't said anything at all and he had only imagined it? Blood pounded in his ears; desire too could be experienced as pain. He was hallucinating, surely. She had said nothing.

But then she was in his arms. He felt a moment of trepidation. This was his work place, he must keep it separate from everything else. At the same time, another part of him felt delight at breaking his own taboo and finally capitulating to fantasy, for other patients had stirred something like this in him before, on this same table. And so he continued, on the stiff sheets smelling of bleach, in the bright antiseptic light. Her breasts were so white and much fuller than he'd imagined, falling out of her yellow blouse. His mouth was on them, biting, her hips rising to his, both of them crying out together.

As they lay on the table afterwards, flushed and surprized, he was mortified. Clara Weiss was all wrong for him, she was too Jewish, too conventional and uneducated. With too much frizzy red hair and far too much sincerity. This was Jacob's mother, after all. Suddenly he had a flash of Magda in her hand-embroidered silk kimono, laughing, "The little widow, darling? But how gallant of you," and he cringed.

Meanwhile, Clara was stroking his head and covering his face with delicate kisses. Thank God she wasn't talking, because he had absolutely no idea what to say to her. But soon he would have to say something, and then he would have to do something. What? What could he possibly do or say now? Reaching across Clara, he glanced at his wristwatch. Ah, he was saved; he had a legitimate excuse to get away! He kissed her back firmly once on the lips, sat up, discretely buttoned his trousers, and declared, "I'm late for a meeting at the hospital, so I'll call you a cab, shall I?"

She blushed. Was she embarrassed? He certainly was. He heard himself giving her instructions for dressing the wound, he heard himself tell her she was lovely, that he would never forget this day. He heard himself say goodbye, and he meant it.

Not Vienna

June, July, and August: Ned still lingered in London. He had been unable to say goodbye after all, unable to go to Vienna as he'd hoped and planned. Herr Rose sent him a letter saying not to come this year because life was becoming too dangerous for the Jews. The putsch might be over but the Nazis, or at least their sympathizers, were everywhere. In March there had been anti-Jewish riots throughout the city. Those ignorant thugs had even marched on the Opera House. But someday soon things would change, he was sure, and their beloved Vienna of song, their Vienna of coffee houses and camaraderie, would return. There was a joke going around that Ned would appreciate, he wrote: "One day soon, Hitler will show up at our coffee house, down at heel, and look for newspapers to read, and we'll say, 'Isn't he that fellow Hitler, that nebbish?' And he will come to our table and ask, 'Excuse me, is *Die Presse* free?' And I will say, 'Not for you, Herr Hitler; not for you!'"

Clara could not understand why this was funny. She had never experienced the leisurely rituals of café life, so she wasn't amused by the stereotype of the scruffy habitué borrowing papers, an aimless hanger-on, a nobody. Every minute of her time had to be accounted for. So once her stitches were out and her wound healed, she had been compelled to come up with a new excuse to visit Dr. Abraham. She decided to have migraines. This seemed reasonable, and it also accounted for her distraction, her loss of appetite, her insomnia. Alice, who frequently endured blinding headaches, was sympathetic — "Now you know how I suffered all those years" — and Clara agreed, yes, she was sorry, she had never realized how awful it could be.

At first Ned would book special hours for their appointments, asking Miss Salmon, who was too well bred to query his instructions, to go home early. They moved from the examination room to his study, where the worn velvet sofa was more inviting and they were less vulnerable to discovery. Then they got greedy and Clara began to require trips to "a specialist" — long trips, and surprisingly frequent. She left the children at home with Millie or occasionally dropped them off with Alice, who was starting to get suspicious as she saw her normally placid sister run to the bus, shouting over her shoulder that she would be back within three hours, make sure Evvie and Danny take a nap after lunch in this heat. Alice sometimes asked Clara, "How is that attractive Dr. Abraham doing?" in order to watch the telltale blush creep up her sister's neck.

But with Ned, Clara was shameless. At a discreet hotel in Richmond they went through the formalities at the desk and walked up the thickly carpeted stairs in silence, as though nothing significant were about to happen. Once the door closed behind them, however, their hunger was mutual and intemperate. Clara had never experienced such urgency of

desire before. Sex had become another reality with its own
landscape, one they entered with open eyes, so as to miss
no instant of beauty or peril. For though they were practi-
cally strangers (or perhaps because of that), they understood
each other wordlessly, anticipating and fulfilling each other's
rhythms as though each joint and muscle and angle and curve
had been designed for no other purpose. She had never been
cherished like this except when her babies were nursing. With
Ned's mouth at her breast, she couldn't help but make the
comparison, though it troubled her to do so. He consumed
her the same way, as though he would die if she refused him.
Still, in spite of his insatiability, he always insisted that she
come first. He never let go until he was sure she was satisfied.
Afterwards he always fell asleep, leaving her alone, grateful,
and lost in this new country of desire.

As soon as he awoke, however, Ned's thoughts flew to Vienna, where he would someday walk the streets again, a free
man. Indeed, he spoke to Clara of Vienna as of a rival lover,
shutting his eyes to the musty pink chintz of the hotel room
and the insistent presence of the woman beside him, her slack
belly with its freckles and stretch marks. He summoned in
their place brilliant anonymous facades, the glitter of street-
lamps on cobblestones, and strange eyes meeting his across
smoky restaurants, under gilded vaults, in mirrors. How he
longed to lose himself in a crowd again. To be without history, the history he had so fervently rejected, which he now
found himself embracing every time Clara was in his arms.

Clara was impatient with this other love. She made little
distinction between Austria and Germany, since Hitler had
spent many years in Vienna and it was there that he learned

to hate Jews. Every Friday she read *The Jewish Chronicle,* and every Friday the reports of Nazi cruelty got longer, more detailed, more surreal. One week the mad propagandist Julius Streicher was spreading the blood libel in *Der Stürmer*; the next, he was warning German maidens about predatory Jewish abductors lying in wait down country lanes. Meanwhile Hitler's mouthpiece, the *Völkischer Beobachter,* was solemnly considering whether a hound owned by Jews ought to be allowed to compete against Aryan dog-hood, and ruling that the master's breed polluted that of his pet.

Surely all this was nonsense to any sane person? But such nonsense had consequences, real and heavy as a bludgeon against a skull, sharp as a beard pulled out by the roots. If windows were smashed, they could always be reglazed. If graves were vandalized, the dead would still rest in peace. But now ordinary Germans were being imprisoned on the flimsiest excuses and held without trial, only to be shot "while attempting to escape" or even "committing suicide" in prison. Jews rushed straight home from work (if they were still lucky enough to have work); their children were ridiculed daily in schools, where the *ABC of Race* instructed:

> *The people hope one day to see the time*
> *When shooting the last Jew will be no crime.*

Despite her horror, Clara could not stop reading. She took to buying the *Manchester Guardian* because its German coverage was more thorough and less neutral than any of the London papers. Every day she feared the worst — not just another shop closed or another journalist arrested, but degradation, torture, and murder. Death was breathing down her neck and she no longer felt safe. She even thought seriously about moving to Canada to join her brother Arthur. Nonetheless, she was careful not to confront Ned too directly with her fears. She knew he would see her as hysterical and pour the disdain of centuries of European civilization on her peasant foreboding. So she kept her observations impersonal.

"Every time there's a diplomatic encounter, we capitulate. First they build up their air force, and we say, 'Well, that's a bit naughty, but since you've already begun, carry on,' and then we let them have conscription, and now we say, 'Fine, go ahead, build submarines. We don't care if they're bigger, better, or faster than ours, as long as you have fewer.' It's ridiculous! I don't understand why the League of Nations can't enforce sanctions against Germany. That's its whole purpose, isn't it? To prevent rearmament?"

"Yes, in theory. But don't forget, a lot of people have a very bad conscience about the way we treated Germany after the war, and they feel it's only fair to let the Germans rebuild. I have to admit, I understand that point of view. I've spent a lot of time over there and seen how bad things are. Germany was a country famous for poetry and music and philosophy, and now its people can barely get by."

"But they aren't making poetry and music and philosophy, Ned, they're murdering Jews," she cried, unable to keep calm. "Doesn't anybody see the difference?"

"No von has effer cared vot heppens to zee Jews, Frau Veiss. We all know that, even here in England. We never belong anywhere, that's the problem. You know that as well as I do. The Germans don't see Jews as part of their Germany and we blame them, but do the English see us as part of their England?"

"It is not the same here. Jews aren't being killed in England."

"No, not at the moment. But some people, like Oswald Mosely's crowd, are headed that way. And I grew up not far from the site of the medieval massacre of Jews at York, so I'm not impressed by all the sanctimony on the BBC."

What was happening in Germany became a kind of counterpoint to their affair. First they would make love, then they would argue, equally passionately, about politics. June, July, August: they scoured the papers for insights on foreign affairs and debated every decision of the Conservative government. MacDonald had finally resigned, but Baldwin seemed equally inadequate to the times. Was he for peace or for security? Could one be for both? Clara and Ned could not decide.

"I agree with you, diplomacy doesn't work with fanatics. They only understand power," he said. "Really, what we need is a hero. Someone should just shoot the man, before it's too late!"

"But then we'd just be reducing ourselves to his level."

"Don't tell me you've signed the peace pledge. Look Clara, either Hitler's a terrible threat or he's not. Either we take action or we don't."

"But isn't there's some middle ground between violence and passivity?" They had had this argument too many times, and there didn't seem to be a resolution to it. Politics was spoiling their pleasure. She wanted to get dressed, to go for a walk, to have a cup of tea in the pretty garden of the hotel. Maybe they could get some sandwiches as well. She felt hollow. Months of craving Ned had carved away the modest padding of maternity. Her hipbones jutted; she hadn't felt this light, this unencumbered, since before the children were born.

"My father tried to find that middle ground most of his life, but he finally gave up. All the waiting and waiting for things to change just eats away at you, when you know what's right but can't do anything about it."

"It must have been frustrating for him." She pressed her lips against his shoulder. His skin was dusky and smooth and a heat came from him. His chest hairs were moss: soft and curly, sweet smelling. Lying next to him was like sunning herself on a rock.

His eyes were fixed on the ceiling and he did not respond to her caress. He was never able to talk to her and touch her at the same time; indeed, he hardly even looked at her while speaking. Just as he played music with closed eyes, so he needed to concentrate on the words he was shaping, as though they too were music. On the other hand, he liked to make love with his eyes open, which unnerved her at first. Leonard, shy Leonard, had always squeezed his shut no matter how dark the room.

Clara mused idly that seeing was like touching, while hearing was like being touched. Seeing was so active, reaching out to the busy world or withdrawing from it by opening or shutting the eyes. But hearing was passive, enduring equally the kiss and the slap, the whisper and the shout. Unable to close its ear-lids. As now, when Ned was still talking.

"The world fell short of what he believed it could be. Should be. And I think we disappointed him too. I was more interested in music, Alta liked the boys, Mama just wanted a quiet life."

"Well, I can understand that. Can't you?"

"Of course. But the problem was that nothing but his ideal world seemed real to him. Sometimes he'd be reading me a bedtime story, full of enthusiasm, doing all the different voices, but I could tell his real self was somewhere else. I could rub my face against his prickly tweed jacket and smell his stinky Russian tobacco, but he wasn't really there."

Why was he telling her things he'd never spoken of to anyone but Alta in his whole life? Clara listened with such intensity he couldn't help himself, but he knew he'd regret it later. He was breaking all his rules with her.

For her part, Clara encouraged his reminiscences, flattered that he would confide in her. But although recalling childhood sorrows was better than talking about the present anguish in Germany, it still displaced the intimacy between them. What she really wanted to talk about was what was going on now, in her life and his. Especially her hopes and fears for Jacob, and how this relationship would affect him. Especially the future of this relationship.

"Where did he go?" she asked, back up on her elbows, eyes like spring rain on his face.

"Oh, he went off to fight the Bolshevik Revolution. Not quite the battle His Majesty's government had in mind, I'm afraid. We had letters from him for a few months, mostly asking for money and supplies for the comrades. And then there was nothing. My mother wrote to all his cronies. She even visited the consulate in London. But nobody knew anything."

"Nothing at all? And you never heard from him again? Oh Ned, I didn't realize! At least, with Jake we knew. It was horrible, he was dead, but we knew. But not to know what happened. How could you bear it?"

"Well, we heard rumours, but they all contradicted each

other. He was on a secret mission, or he had been badly wounded blowing up a train, or he was in prison — you know the kind of thing. One man, a distant cousin, claimed to have seen him on the road, disguised as a peddler, selling icons from village to village to ferret out sympathizers for the cause. We really liked the idea of his being a spy because it kept him alive and important for a while longer. But we never heard from him again."

Ned sat up, lit a cigarette and breathed smoke out slowly.

"Actually, you know, precious few of those men came back from Russia. Only those who could prove they had fought for the Allies were allowed to return. Some of the others finally sent for their wives and children, but Papa knew my mother would never have joined him."

"I would have, if it were you," Clara said.

A jolt like electricity in his chest. He hated it when she talked like this, as though what was between them really existed, permanently, in the outside world.

"That's easy to say now, but just think about it for a moment. First of all, Mama had been very happy to leave there. Second, she had a good job. Then, Alta and I had no real connection to Russia, we couldn't even speak the language. To us, Russia was just history, and most of that history was pretty unattractive. We'd heard too many stories about pogroms, about people being beaten up or starved or what-have-you, to want to go there. So he had to go alone. He couldn't expect us to share his dreams."

"Then he should have given them up. His children were more important."

Red spots stood out on Clara's cheekbones, giving her a clownish, crazed look. He felt a sudden distaste for her relentless maternity.

"A man who gives up his dreams has nothing, Clara. Nothing. I still think my father was a hero. He did what was necessary."

Ned stubbed out the cigarette with unnecessary force, then got up to pour himself a glass of water. He let the tap run until it was really cold, then moved to the window and pulled the heavy rose-flowered curtain aside. Only one o'clock, but the sky had greyed for a storm; the tall poplars lining the drive whipped back and forth and the hotel garden was deserted, a few tea things abandoned on a table, a single chair overturned. Somewhere a dog barked discordantly. He sipped slowly, his mind already back at work, then began to gather up his clothes.

"Look Clara, I've got a lot to do this afternoon. Let's go, shall we?"

When she didn't reply, he turned around to find her sobbing quietly into her pillow, going too far as usual.

"Oh Lord. *Now* what's the matter?"

"Sorry," her muffled voice replied. "It's just . . . I miss my father too, you know, and Jacob lost Leonard, and there's too much of it, that's all."

Frustration at all she was not allowed to say and shame at revealing herself once again as a sentimental woman made her cry even harder.

"Too much of what?"

"I don't know. Losing people, I guess. Men disappearing."

"It's always been like that. That's history. That's human nature."

"I can't believe it's human nature for a father to abandon his children."

"Much worse things happen every single day. They're happening right now with the Nazis, for God's sake!"

"But you'll never get over losing your father. And Jacob will never get over losing Leonard."

"He will, eventually. Don't worry about Jacob, Clara. He's much stronger than you think. He's got a good head on his shoulders and lots of talent. What more does anyone need?"

"I don't know how to describe it. It's something inside, a security you get from being loved properly."

"And what makes you think he doesn't have that?"

"All he's got is me, and I'm so busy with the little ones all the time. I can't even help him with his music. I'm just not good enough." .

"He has other people to help him with his music. That's not what he needs from you, Clara. You're his mother. All that matters is that you love him. Besides, he has lots of happy memories of his father. Jacob will be fine."

"But you don't think too much is expected of him?"

"We all have to grow up. He's just doing it a little faster than some."

Ned had finished dressing and started handing Clara her things. Pretty dress, this: a sage green silk that brought out the colour of her eyes. Was it new?

"Thank you for listening, Ned. It means a lot to me to be able to talk about Jacob. About all the children."

He didn't answer, so she went on recklessly. "Sometimes I get so tired of being alone. Don't you?"

Straightening his tie, he saw the reflection of her strained white face and wild red hair in the mirror. This conversation was definitely getting out of hand; he'd better cut it short right away.

"Actually, I wish I had more time alone. But, alas, I have to rush back to work where at least a dozen people will complain that I'm late. Then they'll cough in my face, cry on my shoulder, share the intimate details of their digestive tracts, and make me miss my tea. So please, dearest Clara, may we go now?"

Clara forced herself to smile and sat up to brush her hair, which was as tangled as her thoughts. He had shut her up again. He always did. He always had to be in control, and although he was the soul of courtesy, he somehow managed to diminish her in the process. But she couldn't go on keeping Ned and her children in separate compartments. She couldn't go on pretending all she wanted from him was sexual pleasure and not daily support and companionship.

The clandestine nature of their affair had once seemed so right. In the first delirium of desire, she had needed a happiness apart from her children. More than that: a happiness that patently excluded them, which she could keep to herself greedily and not share, like the bar of dark chocolate she hid under her stockings for late nights, alone. But the long summer had taken the edge off her sexual hunger and sharpened her guilt. These trysts with Ned, which in the beginning felt more real than anything she'd ever known, had become too detached from life at home to satisfy her.

Still, she was afraid that if she confronted him directly she might lose him. And she wasn't ready to face that possibility yet. Since she'd found Ned, her life had become so much bigger. She couldn't bear the thought of it contracting down to four walls, to baths and meals and lessons, to shopping and bills and laundry and nothing else, nothing really for her, again.

After school ended in July, the summer had stretched ahead of Jacob interminably. There was nothing to do except hang around the house reading or practising the piano or wander over to the park to play football or some other stupid game. Meanwhile, his mother seemed odder than ever, at once distracted and abrasive. She was always forgetting when their library books were due or what she needed at the grocer's after they'd walked all the way there with Danny straggling behind whining that he was thirsty. Then she'd either scold them in front of everyone or impulsively buy them whatever they wished — ice cream or cake or sweets — even though it was right before dinner. He disliked the randomness of their days and longed for the return of school and predictability.

He was also troubled by his mother's headaches and her frequent trips to the doctor. She said it was nothing, but that's what Papa had said about the pain in his belly before they found the cancer. Only once did he reveal how scared he was, and Clara responded with such extravagant guilt that he never brought it up again. But Jacob continued to watch her furtively for signs of disease. Surely she was getting thinner?

To get away from his worries, he started to spend more time with his friend Nathaniel. Nathaniel attended the same cheder as Jacob did, though his family was more orthodox. There were seven children crammed into a little terrace house, a bearded solemn father who worked late every night, a shy mother always busy in the kitchen. Heavy meals, heavy smells, patched clothes, darned stockings. But there was order, there were rules and expectations about everything and the main expectation for Nathaniel was that he should study. He and Jacob were treated like princes; all the other children had to shush when they were studying. But the little ones were indulged when Nathaniel's father came home. He gently interviewed each of the children about his or her day, and then he read them all a story.

At his own house, Jacob no longer listened to stories, though he liked to read them to Evvie and Danny. But at Nathaniel's it was different; the low murmurous masculine voice, like water running over stones, soothed something deep inside him. An ache that had diminished during the two months he'd practised Mozart with Dr. Abraham had revived with increased vigour now that their practice sessions had ended.

He'd only seen Dr. Abraham once since then. Toward the end of June, Ned took him out for tea. He'd driven up in a beautiful new Triumph saloon car, not quite as swish as Aunt Alice's Daimler but much sportier. Just the kind of car Jacob wanted to buy when he became a man: different from all the boring Austins and Morrises out there, but not so fancy that people would stare. Then they'd gone to a restaurant where each table had a heap of tiny crustless sandwiches and a lovely silver pyramid of iced cakes and you could eat as much as you liked of everything. A waiter in a white jacket kept appearing mysteriously and pouring tea. Jacob had been afraid he was being greedy, but Dr. Abraham didn't mind. He said he remembered how hungry he'd always been at Jacob's age.

"Dr. Abraham?"

"Yes, Jacob?"

"Can I ask you something personal? Mum says I shouldn't ask personal questions, that it's rude, but I don't really understand why. I mean, why isn't it rude to ask someone what he thinks of the government, but it's rude to ask him what he likes to eat?"

"Sometimes you sound like a rabbi, Jacob. I think you're spending far too much time splitting hairs at that Hebrew school of yours. But fine, ask away."

"Do you like my mother?"

"Do I like your *mother*?"

Maybe he had been rude after all, since Dr. Abraham took such a long time to answer. But when he finally spoke, he didn't sound too annoyed.

"Now that is a funny question. But of course I do, she's a very nice lady. Why do you ask?"

"I was just curious. Because she doesn't have a lot of friends, and since my father died, she's alone all the time."

"Maybe she likes being alone. Don't you?"

"Sometimes. Because there aren't many people I really like."

"That's how I am too. And perhaps your mother's the same way."

"I guess so. But I worry about her. I mean, it was my father's job to take care of her and he's gone, so it seems like it's my job now."

"Good lord, Jacob, it's not your job."

"But you take care of your mother."

"That's different."

"Why?"

"Because you're just a boy. I'm grown up already."

"How old were you when your father went away?"

"I was thirteen, but don't forget I had a big sister to take care of me."

"I don't ever want to lose anyone else. I want to be a famous musician and get really rich and buy a huge house and keep all my family in it forever. So that even if I travel far away, they'll always be there when I come back."

Ned laughed. "That doesn't sound very fair. You get to have all the fun and they have to sit at home waiting for you?"

"Well, maybe they could travel too. Maybe I'll take Danny along with me, for company. And you could come too, if you like."

"I tell you what, Jacob. You get famous first and then you invite me. I promise I'll come."

Remembering this conversation made Jacob happy. It also made him lonely, so he asked his mother if they might invite the doctor to tea at their house again, and she'd said they would, someday soon, but then did nothing. He thought of telephoning Dr. Abraham himself, but he was too shy to attempt it. And since Miss Westerham always went to Brighton for the whole month of August, he felt quite abandoned.

Mozart had begun to irritate him because the music seemed so frivolous. These days Jacob preferred Bach, the more difficult and precise the better. Hours and hours he hammered away at the intransigent cliffs of *The Well-Tempered Clavier*. That Bach wrote most of these pieces for his oldest son, Wilhelm Friedemann, did not escape his attention; indeed, it fed a melancholy determination to master all forty-eight preludes and fugues someday.

Bach had declared that these pieces were intended "for the use and profit of the musical youth desirous of learning as well as for the pastime of those already skilled." Which was Jacob? Both, he supposed. Though these days not so much desirous of learning as of *becoming* music, so he could shut out everything else. But it was hard to become one with the piano. It could not be an extension of the shoulder and

arm like the violin or of the lungs and lips like the flute. It
was too big, too self-contained, to embody impulses already
inside the musician and simply incarnate them in another
shape. Instead, he had to adapt to the piano, a frighteningly
complex instrument consisting of thousands of parts: hammers, pedals, levers, keys; ivory, felt, metal, wood.

How many parts does the human body have? Each hand
alone has twenty-seven bones, bones with the names of Byz-
antine priests: the scaphoid, the semilunar, the cuneiform,
the unciform, the os magnum. Yet the keyboard is the only
instrument on which each finger and thumb can play a separate and distinct note at the same time, or the full hand
is articulated, a polyphony of ten. The only instrument in
which both hands are equals against the forgiving asymmetry
of nature.

Clara could see how lost Jacob felt, but she was convinced
that having Ned in the house right now would be a mistake. She needed certain boundaries in her life, and the one
between her children and danger was inviolable. Until this
relationship was better defined, it threatened her domestic
peace. If she had felt comfortable telling Jacob the truth, it
might have been different, but it was too soon to get him
involved. For one thing, he seemed to feel that Ned was his
own special friend, and her involvement with the man he
idolized might not, in fact, be welcome. For another, if she
and Ned separated he would lose another father, and she
couldn't bear to do that to him.

So no, Clara couldn't tell Jacob. And not only that, she'd
have to be very careful not to leave any clues to alert him

to the situation. It was clear that she hadn't been vigilant enough so far, for her sister had figured out what was going on. Damn Alice! Her stolid conventionality usually made her sniff out scandal even where there wasn't any, but this time she was right.

Still, although Clara wanted to protect the children, she couldn't understand why she and Ned had to hide from everyone else. Neither of them was married. Why shouldn't they be seen together? Couldn't they go out in public once in a while, to a concert or for a meal? At other times, she knew that it was too late; their relationship was illicit and would be recognized as such at once. Flames danced about them, and anyone who came close must surely be singed. She also suspected that Ned despised the social niceties ordinary courtship entailed. She could just imagine them somewhere, sitting primly, trying not to touch each other, while people fluttered up, twittering, "Dr. Abraham! How nice to see you. And who is your lovely companion?" Oh no, she knew he wouldn't tolerate that.

But she resented the secrecy. She wanted to go out somewhere wonderful as a couple. She'd already bought fashionable new clothes to wear just for him, to be a lady and not just a mother. She'd been half-asleep for so long, stumbling after her sick husband and her babies, at everyone else's beck and call. Now she wanted to enjoy herself. More than that, she wanted to travel. She wanted to visit Paris and Florence and Rome; she wanted to hear wonderful music and see wonderful paintings. The Louvre, she'd never been to the Louvre — she'd never been anywhere. With Ned by her side, the life she'd always dreamed of, the life no one else in her family had known she wanted, suddenly seemed possible.

Her parents had been preoccupied by meals, bodily

functions, and the weather; by the price of flour and the cleanliness of floors. Clara loved them but knew this couldn't be all there was. The books she read, the music she heard, the paintings she visited in the National Gallery on Sunday, all these things spoke to her of a passionate engagement with the world she was determined, somehow, someday, to experience for herself. Then she met Leonard at synagogue. He was quiet, contemplative, a lover of books and of nature, a person whose interests lay entirely outside himself. He never talked about his digestion; indeed, he barely noticed food at all. This in itself was marvellously liberating, at least before their marriage, before they slept together and Clara realized how abstemious all his appetites were. But the major attraction for her was that Leonard took her seriously. He let her talk and did not belittle her dreams.

At the same time, her parents approved of him because he was a good Jewish boy, responsible, working with his father. So Clara went away with Leonard Weiss, joint proprietor of Weiss and Son Dry Goods, Bell Lane, who cherished her, gave her three children, and then left her all alone, as she had always been, with no one who really knew her.

Clara justified her daydreams of a future with Ned by reminding herself that she deserved some pleasure after everything she'd gone through. Besides, he was already so fond of Jacob; surely, in time, he would express an interest in her other children? But the one time she had dared to ask him if he'd ever thought of getting married, he'd responded elliptically.

"Have you read Henry James?"

"A little," she replied. "But I have to confess I find him rather tedious. That endless analysis of people's slightest thoughts . . . well, *my* life has always gone by much quicker than that, I'm afraid. And if I took that long to worry things out, if I were that scrupulous, I'd never get anything done."

He laughed appreciatively, then went on. "Actually, what I was thinking of was a story called 'The Lesson of the Master.' Do you know it?"

"No, I'm afraid not."

"A character in it says that one has no business having any children if one wants to accomplish anything artistic. I've always believed that."

"I suppose it depends whether you think the highest purpose of life is art," Clara replied, after a pause in which a wave of desolation swept over her and then away, somewhere else. A distant beach seen from a cliff once, on holiday in Cornwall. For he was only talking about having children, not about getting married. After all, they needn't have any more children. She already had three.

"Well, don't you?"

"To be honest, I'm not sure. I mean, I've often felt frustrated, especially with my painting. I know I could have gone much farther with it, experimented and improved, if I hadn't been home with children."

She paused, not sure how much she wanted to reveal her hidden aspirations. Perhaps he would think her vain and silly? But he had admired her paintings, after all.

"I would have loved to have travelled like you have, to have gone abroad and seen the great galleries of Europe: the Uffizi, the Louvre, the Prado . . . well, *you* know, I'm sure you've been to them all."

Ned nodded, feeling a bit uncomfortable. Compared to her he was extraordinarily privileged.

"Of course I've seen the pictures in books, but it's not the same as seeing them up close and experiencing the texture of the paint, how the colours change with the light, the true proportions of things," she continued. "I even had a fantasy of going to art school abroad, but I knew my parents would never let me go. They thought of painting as a ladylike hobby, not as something serious, and I wasn't brave enough to challenge them. And anyway, I got married so young, and then a year later I had Jacob."

She laughed somewhat bitterly. "You know, I look at Jacob now, and he seems like such a little boy at twelve. But I was only six years older when I walked down the aisle on my father's arm."

"Do you feel that you've missed out on your vocation, then?"

"I don't think I'd put it quite like that. You never know if you're really any good, do you? Although there are always moments when it seems possible, even now . . . But anyhow, could any painting I might have made be as precious as my children are? Never! Of that I am sure."

"Well, then, you made the right choice," he said, and began to undo her blouse.

"Ned, I'm serious about this."

"So am I," he replied. "Why do you women always have so many buttons on your clothes?"

Finally, at the end of August, Ned asked how Jacob was doing.

Clara's heart leapt. Perhaps her two worlds could come together, for the tension of keeping them apart was becoming unendurable.

"He's been having a rotten time, I'm afraid," she replied. "There's not much for him to do here in the summer, but I couldn't afford to take the children to the seaside this year. I think he's very glad school is starting up again soon. He's not a boy who likes to be idle."

"Is he keeping on with his music?"

"Oh yes, he's gone mad about Bach, practises for hours and hours."

"Good for him, that's the best stuff."

"Do you think so? Why? I mean, Bach's lovely of course, but it's all so regular, you know. He used to prefer pieces that were very dramatic, with lots of changes in dynamics and in tempo. And now he's like a little metronome."

"It's important to get a solid foundation of technique first, and not just cover up sloppy playing with bravura displays of emotion," Ned replied firmly.

"You sound like you're quoting somebody else. Probably somebody German, with a pointy beard and a very serious expression."

He laughed. "Do I? Sorry. I didn't mean to be pompous. My sister Alta used to tease me about that. Sometimes she called me 'Headward.'

Clara clapped her hands, delighted that he would share a joke at his own expense. Carried forward on this wave of good humour, Ned continued, "How would it be if I took Jacob to a concert, then? I think he deserves a treat after so much hard work."

"Oh, he would be thrilled. You have no idea how much he's missed you and how hard it's been for me seeing that. I've felt so guilty, like I've stolen you away from him, in a way."

"Well, I've missed him too," Ned spoke hastily, cutting her off. Although they'd never talked openly about it, he'd felt compelled to give Jacob up because of their affair. The one time he'd taken the boy out, in June, he'd actually asked

Ned if he liked Clara. Ned didn't know whether this was childish clairvoyance or just coincidence, but it unnerved him. It was impossible to keep seeing the boy while sleeping with his mother.

Now he woke up each morning with a nebulous sense of disappointment, an old familiar malaise that had dissipated during the months he and Jacob had played music together. Their friendship had been something very precious. Ned had felt oddly young again talking to the boy, as though he too were discovering things for the first time. He caught a glimpse of his face in the hotel mirror. The face of a stranger looked back, a tender smile playing about his lips. Who was this man who loved children? No one he thought he knew.

"Why are you smiling?" Clara asked.

"Oh, nothing important," he replied. "Just thinking."

But the following week, a letter arrived at the Weiss house, requesting the pleasure of the company of Master Jacob Weiss, accompanied by his mother, to attend a concert the first Sunday in October at St. Martin's in the Fields. The favour of a reply would be appreciated.

Jacob was over the moon. He'd never actually been to a real grownup concert before, only to student recitals. To hear full-time musicians playing for people who paid for the privilege — to sit with such people, people who really understood what they were hearing. It must be a different world. At first he wondered whether there would be any other children there, but then he decided it didn't really matter because he too was, or intended to be, a professional musician, so he belonged in such a setting.

Nathaniel's father had told him music was not a proper vocation for a Jewish boy, that all the travel and late hours were not conducive to a respectable home life and dedication to Torah. But Johann Sebastian Bach, the greatest musician of all time, had a respectable home life. And he was very religious; more religious, though he was a Christian, than Jacob. He even had twenty children! So maybe it was possible. Not that Jacob wanted twenty children. Since talking to Dr. Abraham, he wasn't sure he wanted any.

It would be nice to talk to Dr. Abraham again, to sit between him and Clara, as he had at the spring concert when they'd played the Mozart. Ned all dark and bristly, Clara all fair and soft, and himself in the middle. Held by them, and by the music.

He couldn't wait.

Autumn 1935 – Spring 1936

Equal Temperament

A *gravicembalo col piano e forte* was presented by Bartolommeo Cristofori of Padua to Prince Ferdinando dei Medici in 1709. The strings of this new instrument were not plucked, like the harpsichord's, but hit with a hammer, so the musician could play louder or softer at will. At first, this instrument spanned only four and a half octaves, but over time its range and expressiveness grew until it became the seven-and-a-half-octave pianoforte in Clara Weiss's sitting room.

When Jacob's finger depresses a piano key, the far end tilts up, raising a lever that connects to a felt-tipped hammer, throwing that hammer forward to hit the appropriate string. When Jacob's finger releases the key, a felt pad, called a damper, drops back onto the string and stops the vibration. And when his foot depresses the right pedal it raises all the dampers so that the strings can keep sounding to infinity — or at least beyond human apprehension. If you open up his piano, you can see that the strings form a beautifully tuned harp hidden in the belly of the instrument. That is, Jacob's piano is really a stringed instrument like Ned's violin. But its mechanism is a lot more complicated, involving not just a single bow but many levers and dampers and hammers; not only the hands, but the feet.

Jacob performs these actions instantaneously, fluidly, swaying a little from the waist, his elbows lifted from his body like wings, his eyes flickering over the music, not so much reading as scanning a crowd for familiar faces. Sometimes he hums, anticipating the melody to be summoned by his fingers, encouraging the notes to take their places. Humming keeps him from scrutinizing what he's doing with his eyes and elbows and fingers and feet. If he thinks too much the notes mask themselves, whirling past in a crazy dance, shouting questions over their shoulders, and he can't hear, can't see, can't keep up.

It is one of those days. The music resists him, utterly. He tries to slow it down, to coax it back, to be gentle. But it stalks away, offended, because his attention wavered. He abandoned his hands too soon and the music is affronted. Tears gather in his eyes. He is not good enough; he will never be good enough. The piano can do this to him, and he hates it.

Evvie was the first to notice something was wrong. Before Millie, on her knees scrubbing the tiles in the entry; before Clara, half-asleep as she always was these days, dreaming with eyes open. But no one listened when she said Danny didn't look right. After all, Evvie had been born a worrier. It was a family joke that she was the White Queen in miniature, crying before the needle pricked her finger, fretting about things before they even happened.

Nevertheless, when she thought about it later, Clara realized that some residually alert part of her had noticed that her youngest child felt hot, that he complained more than usual of being tired and staggered a bit when he walked; some part of her meant to do something about it. But she didn't. When he'd cried that his tummy hurt, she just told him he'd been eating too many sweets and ran off to Ned, to take her pleasure. And came home later to a house full of tears and misery, for Millie, unable to reach her, had called Aunt Alice, who had called for an ambulance, and Danny had been sent to the hospital with acute appendicitis. Now Evvie was crying, her narrow face more pinched than usual, and Jacob was furious with her (or more furious than usual), and she had to leave again at once to go to the hospital, beside herself with guilt and grief, begging the cabby to drive faster.

How could she have failed her son this way? She who had hovered over his cot through every infant cough and fever, who dozed with sick children in her lap night after night rather than abandon them to their clammy beds. She had abandoned them all, somehow. She had reneged on the contract she signed the day each child was born, to put them first. And she ought to have known better. If you relaxed your vigilance for even a moment, you were punished. It was the one infallible law of Clara's world.

At the hospital, Alice was still in charge. It was rare that she accomplished anything that justified her innate sense of self-importance but today reality coincided with fantasy. Today she really was essential, her instincts were right, she did know more than other people gave her credit for. And feeling vindicated after a lifetime of being underestimated made her generous. Her sister forbore to ask Clara where she had been or even to hint that her mysterious errand might have involved a certain handsome violinist. In fact, Alice seemed almost to want to keep Clara from confessing. She just chattered on and on about how she'd known at once it was appendicitis because the same thing had happened to her Roger when he was ten, and the doctor back then had told her that the boy might well have died had it not been for her quick thinking. Perhaps it was nothing more than mother's instinct, not that she meant to imply that Clara wasn't a good mother, but you know what I mean, don't you, dear?

Meanwhile Clara's thoughts raced round and round a track with no exit. She said thank you a dozen times, congratulated her sister on her percipience, and berated herself. At last Alice bustled off, having been sufficiently appreciated, and a fog of silence moved in.

Clara felt terror beyond anything she had ever experienced. This was not the same as when Leonard was ill. She had been just as helpless then, but not responsible as she was responsible now, despite what the doctor told her: that it was not her fault, that the symptoms were easily mistaken for those of an ordinary stomach ache, that she did not wait too long. She had waited too long, and she would never forgive herself.

She sat by her youngest child, still unconscious after surgery, holding his hand, praying, and not forgiving herself. Doctors and nurses came and went, carrying odd bits of rubber tubing, bottles with large important labels, instruments of cold and shining steel: the machinery of an alien planet. The medical personnel asked, then begged, and finally ordered her to get out of the way. This was a recovery ward; she must sit downstairs to wait or, better yet, go home and come back later. Didn't she have other children to look after? It was hospital policy; she must leave at once.

The smell of ether was giving her a headache. Danny was asleep. No one needed her and she felt utterly useless. So finally she capitulated, but from the lobby she called Ned. She asked him to make them let her stay.

"I can't do that," he replied. "Besides, they're right. You'll only be in the way if you hover around, fussing. Believe me, the nurses will make sure Danny's comfortable."

"But it's all my fault, Ned. I wasn't paying attention, I should have seen that he wasn't well. I'm his mother, for God's sake!"

"Of course it's not your fault," he said, soothingly. "It's common to feel that way, but really, appendicitis comes on so fast it's very hard to recognize. Even doctors make mistakes sometimes and miss it, or worse, panic and open up a patient for nothing."

Like Alice, though for different reasons, Ned was oddly happy. What a relief to be just a doctor with Clara. The intensity of their affair had become oppressive, but he hadn't known how to end it. And here was fate offering him an honourable way out; he could be of use to the family as an old friend and at the same time withdraw from Clara as a lover. Right now, she wouldn't have time for him anyway. It was perfect.

"I wish I could believe you. But I'm sure you're just trying to make me feel better so I won't blame you as well as blaming myself. Because if I hadn't been so obsessed with you, with every single minute we could spend together, maybe Danny would never have got so sick in the first place."

Now he was angry. She had no right to blame him for her inability to manage her own life. But he didn't intend to discuss this on the phone, with Clara making a fool of herself in the hospital lobby where everyone could hear her.

"Look, do you want me to come take you home? You sound very upset."

Clara knew from the chill in his voice that she had gone too far. But who else did she have?

"Yes, Ned, please. Please Ned, please come. Please come see my boy. I'm sorry. Of course it's not your fault, it's not anyone's fault."

"It will take me about half an hour to get there. Try to calm down. Why don't you go have a cup of tea while you're waiting? There's a tea room on the main floor."

"Yes, I will. Thank you. Thank you, Ned."

She repeated his name like a charm to keep the connection between them. But he never said hers, not even once. He talked to her as he might talk to anyone. Perhaps he did feel guilty. After he hung up she stood there for a full minute, listening to the dial tone. Was it C? D? E flat? She could no longer tell, though this was a game she had always played with Jacob. The possibility of music was no longer a consolation. She would give it up. She would give up everything if only Danny were well again.

He found her in a corner of the hospital restaurant, hands clenched around a mug of cold tea. She was wearing a rumpled and rather dirty mackintosh, her hair flaming under a green paisley scarf. Her face was very white, and her staring eyes, rimmed with red, looked more green and haunted than ever.

Two tables over, a heavy woman with bleached blond hair was tenderly spooning rice pudding into the mouth of a rigid child in a wheelchair. The child, a girl of perhaps eleven, was painfully emaciated; controlling her mouth long enough to swallow food clearly took every ounce of strength. Her bony arms were strapped to the sides of the chair, and her legs, covered by a blue and yellow plaid blanket, stuck out in front of her, but each frail muscle vibrated with concentration on the labour of love she and her mother had set each other. The mother cooed to her and the girl smiled back. Tears ran down Clara's face as she watched them. Preoccupied, she wasn't aware of Ned's presence until he sat down opposite her.

"Sad sight, isn't it? Cerebral palsy. No possibility of improvement. And for all we know, a fine mind trapped in there, unable to express itself."

"Oh Ned, it's just dreadful. And it must be nearly as bad for the mother, not being able to help."

"Well, at least she's got a mother who loves her. Some children are just dumped here indefinitely and no one visits them."

"How can people be so cruel?"

"Come now, Clara, we've talked about this kind of thing before. There are many degrees of evil in this world. In ancient times, abandoning a damaged child wasn't even on the scale."

They were both quiet for a moment. Clara picked up her cup, but when the cold liquid sloshed against her lips, she put it down again with a grimace.

"Thank you for coming, Ned. I really do appreciate it."

"That's all right, I was glad to help," he replied mildly, trying on his new role. "I've already been to the recovery room and had a look at Danny. He came through the surgery very well. Now he'll just sleep for a few hours until the anaesthetic wears off."

"But the doctor said the infection had started to spread," said Clara.

"Well, that's to be expected with a burst appendix. But

don't worry, they've got things under control. He'll have to stay for a fortnight or so, but you'll be able to visit him often. He'll be fine, I promise you."

Clara recognized that she was being patronized, but she didn't care. He was here: a body beside her to ward off the panic.

"They said I should come back in the morning. It's just that I know he'll wake up in the night and be so terrified. He'll cry for me and I won't be here. And I wasn't here when he came in. Oh Ned, I can't bear it." Tears came again, but she must not lose control in front of him, she must not. He would be so scornful.

And indeed, impatience was creeping into his voice. "How old is he now? Four? Surely he's old enough to get through the night without his mother."

"He's only three. And anyhow, are we ever old enough?"

"What does that mean?"

"Well, there are times when I wish there were somebody to take care of me, somebody who would just be there without me having to ask him or thank him or pay him. You know." Clara laughed, embarrassed at having revealed such weakness.

"Do you think there ever is anyone like that? I don't," he replied, with a bitterness that surprised both of them. "I think it's an illusion children have to grow out of. Parents can't really protect you, even when you're small. There's too much that can go wrong. Look, I know a burst appendix is serious, but he will get better. Other kids don't, not just that girl over there, but worse. I see them die all the time, and no amount of mother-love can help a bit."

"I don't agree with you, Ned. I think it helps a lot. It's the difference between being alone in a crisis and having a hand to hold onto. You may be right, love can't cure the ills of the world, but surely it makes them easier to endure."

"Maybe for some people. I wouldn't know since my family didn't believe in hand holding. Well, never mind. Are you ready to go home?"

"Yes, thank you."

What on earth was she thanking him for? For belittling her situation by reminding her how much worse things were for others and implying that they had actually been worse for him? How much did she really know about him? Or about anyone, for that matter.

Danny would wake alone in the night to cold, scratchy hospital sheets, their smell of starch and infirmity. He would wake to pain and fear. And whatever he was able to tell her about his experience, she would never fully share it, now or later, when its shadow fell on other nights, taking him farther away from her into his own life. So that one day he might sit across from a woman who loved him, as bitter and withdrawn as Ned and as resentful that love had been denied him when he was a child, when he was still young enough to have expected it as his due.

Ned helped her into her dingy coat, took her arm politely, and led her outside. In the relative privacy of the car, she leaned over, flung her arms around his neck, and kissed him with surprising warmth.

"What was that for?" he asked, pulling away to start the ignition.

"For being kind. For coming to help me."

"It was the least I could do."

Ned turned to look at her directly. Her gaze reflected the

image of himself he liked best: a fine upstanding man, a good person, a citizen. Not a shabby outsider in disguise.

"Do you want to go straight home?" he asked, his voice mellow now with desire, despite his earlier resolution to break away from her.

"Yes, I must," Clara replied.

Did he really want her? Their lovemaking earlier that afternoon had been brief and dissatisfying. He had been more preoccupied than usual, rushing to get back to work. And yet he had come to rescue her, albeit reluctantly and with ill grace. She realized once again how hard it was for him to meet her in public, how against his nature to acknowledge their relationship in broad daylight. In a way, his coming to fetch her like this was the greatest intimacy there had ever been between them.

Clara did not go to the concert with Dr. Abraham. She couldn't leave Evvie now, not for a minute, and she felt uncomfortable at the thought of being with Ned, even with Jacob as a chaperone. Keeping away from her lover was the only appropriate punishment for neglecting Danny. So Jacob had to go alone, which he secretly preferred. It was exciting to go out by himself, a taste of the life ahead when he wouldn't have to ask his mother's permission for everything or confide in her if he chose not to.

He polished his shoes until they shone and dressed himself carefully in his recital jacket and tie. Clara tucked a little box of chocolates into his pocket, warning him not to rustle the paper while the music was playing or he would disturb the other concert-goers.

"Don't worry, Mum. I won't embarrass you."

"Oh please, Jacob, don't take that tone with me."

"What tone?"

"You know very well what tone. Haven't I got enough problems right now without you being sarcastic all the time?"

"I am not sarcastic all the time. You're just so touchy these days. Fussing about everything won't make Danny get well any faster, you know."

"Jacob! That was completely uncalled for. I have a good mind to keep you home to teach you a little respect."

"I'm sorry, Mama." He hugged her tight.

She felt so small in his arms now, shrinking as he grew taller, losing all her magical power and authority. They stood silently for a moment, relaxing into this rare embrace, until he asked, "Where's Evvie, anyhow? I want to give her one of these chocolates before I go."

The little girl had been sitting quietly in her favourite chair, the fabric on one arm worn away by her habit of rubbing it while sucking her thumb. Rub, rub, went her fingers, worrying the frayed threads.

"Here I am, Jakey. Can I have one with toffee inside?"

"Yeah, if you can tell which one it is."

Clara contemplated her children as they stood studying the chocolate box. Jacob had to stoop to bring his face down to Evvie's level; he had grown so much recently that his jacket was too short in the sleeves. She knew she had to allow him more freedom, but she didn't know how to let go yet. She realized, unhappily, that all her expertise lay in caring for small children. Adolescents were a mystery to her. Probably this was why nature had decreed that a family needed both a mother and a father.

There was a firm knock at the door, followed immediately

by a second. Ned, at once assertive and understated. He gave her a pleasant impersonal smile and shook both her hand and Evvie's, bowing to the little girl with exaggerated courtesy. Then "Goodbye, we won't be late," and they were gone.

Evvie climbed into her lap with a picture book, contentedly sucking her toffee. Clara settled back into a semblance of the life she knew. Jacob was probably better off with Ned anyway, she reflected, her voice reciting the words on the page while her mind stumbled off in its own direction.

The concert was brilliant. Of course, Jacob would have been delighted to sit in the park and listen to a honking third-rate military band — anything that got him away from the house, any time alone with Dr. Abraham, would have made him more than happy. His life had been so miserable lately that Jacob felt lost. But with Dr. Abraham sitting beside him, black eyes intent on the musicians, he was found again.

Clara would have insisted on holding his hand; she would have whispered banal musical insights to him between movements, disturbing everyone sitting near them, and then shushed him when he replied. But Dr. Abraham just let him be. And for that reason Jacob listened extra hard, so as to be able to discuss the performance properly afterwards. At least one of the cellos was out of tune, the first violinist was amazingly good, and the clarinet came in a fraction of a beat late in the second movement . . . But when they went to tea at a little café around the corner, he found himself talking about something else entirely.

"Dr. Abraham, do you ever miss your father?"

"Of course I do, Jacob. Often."

"Do you think about him when you play music? I mean, do you wish he were there, to hear you perform? Do you think he would have been proud?"

"Oh, I'm sure he would have been. You know, even though my parents didn't get along very well, the one thing they never argued about was my playing the violin. They both loved music so much. I really think it brings out the best in people, don't you?"

"Maybe. Although at school no one cares about music at all. You're only popular if you're good at football or play tricks on the masters. It's so stupid."

"Well, your world right now is pretty small, Jacob. It will get bigger, I promise you. And in the big world, just as many people love music as football. Maybe even more."

"I doubt it. I don't have any friends who play music now."

"Not even one?"

"Not really. There's one other boy in my class who plays the piano and this girl who plays the flute, but neither of them is any good. We had a school recital and it was just pitiful. You should have seen the girls' choir. Half of them couldn't remember the words they were supposed to be singing and the other half were waving at their parents the whole time like complete idiots."

Ned couldn't help laughing, remembering similar events from his own past.

"I think you need to go to a different school then. Somewhere better, where everyone does music and the biggest honour is to be in the choir. I don't know. Dulwich College perhaps."

"Where's that?"

"It's in South London, the other side of the Thames. A grand place, all green fields and towers."

"My mother would never let me go somewhere that far away. And anyhow, we can't afford it."

"Those kinds of schools have scholarships, Jacob. They'd give one to someone as talented as you in a minute."

"Do you really think so?"

"I know so."

"But she'd never let me apply. For years I couldn't even be in any of the Guildhall concerts because I might be too nervous or practice too hard and get sick or something. And my grandfather is always so suspicious of everything that isn't Jewish. You can't imagine what a fuss there was about me being in that Christmas concert. You don't know what they're like."

"I'm sure your family means well, Jacob, but they don't really know how things work in the big world. Would you like me to do a little research for you, make some enquiries and so on? As a friend?"

"You'd do that for me?"

"With pleasure. I really think you're going to go far, Jacob. You have nothing to worry about."

Jacob couldn't help himself. He got up from his seat and gave Ned a big hug. To his surprise and relief, Ned hugged him back. So he rubbed his cheek surreptitiously against the man's chin to feel the pleasant rasp of bristles, something he'd missed for a long, long time.

A wet autumn. Although the fire was going, the house still smelled of mildew, and it made Evvie cough. She put down a fistful of crayons and sighed dramatically.

"I'm bored, Mama. Can't we do something?"

Clara looked up from her sewing. The house looked shabbier than ever, so she was making new curtains in an effort to cheer everyone up. Well, to cheer herself up, anyway, and she'd let Evvie help her pick out the fabric, a William Morris print. It was far too expensive but so lush, all gold and green and endless repetition: a soothing maze.

"You're absolutely right. Boots on! We'll go to Barnes Pond and feed the ducks. You too, Jacob."

"Aw, Mum, feeding ducks is for babies. Besides, I want to finish this book."

"No, my young man, a brisk walk in the fresh air will do you the world of good. You spend far too much time indoors, Jacob. I was just thinking that you ought to take up a sport, football or tennis or swimming, something to build you up a bit. You're looking awfully peaky."

"You've got to be joking! You know I hate all those morons knocking each other down to prove how strong they are."

Clara laughed. He sounded so much like Leonard, who had dismissed physical prowess as evidence of intellectual incapacity.

"Well, we'll discuss this again later. But for now, we need to shake off the cobwebs and get out of the house. Right, Evvie?" she said firmly, knotting a scarf around the little girl's neck.

The bus trundled over Hammersmith Bridge and let them off at Barnes Pond. There was poor old Charlie the goose, a neighbourhood celebrity. Still mourning the death of his mate, he didn't even raise his head from under his wing as they walked past. But no wonder he huddled; the wind was fierce, blowing grit into their faces. A large family of mallards sat puffed up like burst pillows by the edge of the pond, a few hardy souls lumbering to the water with improbable orange feet, bright paddles they tucked under them as soon as they were afloat.

"Other people have the same idea, I guess," said Clara ruefully, observing the litter of bread crusts and sodden cake around the perimeter of the water.

"Everyone feels sorry for them when it's cold," Evvie agreed, her pale pointed face under her black beret giving her the air of a diminutive witch. She tore her crusts into tiny bits and threw them to the ducks, but they didn't even turn their heads to follow the flight of the bread. Only a few seagulls, insatiable as ever, squabbled over who had more, though they hardly swallowed what they fought for.

"This is stupid," said Jacob, kicking at a stone. "We're standing here freezing, and the ducks aren't even hungry."

"Well, if everyone thought the same, and we all stopped feeding them at once, they'd really be in trouble," countered his mother.

"Why? They're part of nature. They lived here before people started pelting them with cake. I'm sure there's other stuff for them to eat."

"Like what?" asked Evvie, her nose running in the cold.

"I don't know. Snails maybe, or worms, or little fish. Just stuff."

"Maybe you're right," said Clara. "But they've been domesticated for so long they probably don't know how to find wild food. Maybe they would just starve if we stopped feeding them."

"Or maybe they'd discover they had amazing inborn duck-like talents," insisted the boy. "They just never get to use them."

"I guess it's all a matter of expectations. If you get used

to having more, it's hard to get by with less. But not necessarily impossible."

"Look, Mama," shouted Evvie. "A different one. What is it?"

"Some kind of seabird. What's it doing on our little pond?"

"Maybe it wanted some cake. Maybe it's having a birthday!" Evvie laughed at her own joke.

"Or maybe it likes to eat fat lazy ducks," added Jacob. "And silly girls who feed them."

Evvie started to cry.

"Jacob!"

"I'm sorry," the boy replied, without conviction.

"It's a cormorant, I think," said Clara. "They usually live right on the coast. And they only eat fish, Evvie, not ducks or little girls."

She gathered her daughter in her arms, lifted her up to kiss the soft cheek, and licked away a single glittering tear. They all stood in silence for a moment, transfixed by the bird's grand disdain. The cormorant had settled on a rock protruding from the water. It spread its black wings once, twice, to shake off the beaded water drops, then stretched its long neck luxuriously, oblivious to the ordinary ducks and geese and gulls cluttering the pond. Equally oblivious to the gawking people. Though it was the misplaced creature, they were the ones who felt like intruders.

"Can we please go now, Mum?" Jacob asked finally, trying to keep the petulance out of his voice.

The dignity of the bird made him ashamed of himself. He ought to be kinder to his mother and sister. They were just as worried about Danny as he was, and with more justification, since they spent a lot more time with him. Jacob hardly ever played with his little brother. Why? He resolved to be less selfish when Danny came home. Maybe he could teach him to play the piano.

"Are you ready to go, sweetheart?" Clara asked the girl, who nestled into her, suddenly so small. With Danny away, the smallest.

"Yes, Mama. Can you make cocoa when we get home, please?"

"Mmm. That's just what the doctor ordered."

And off they went, cold but quieter in spirit, to drink cocoa and eat toast, saving the crusts for their next expedition to feed the birds.

And then, when it was starting to feel like they'd never lived any other way — with an exhausted Clara running between hospital and home, a subdued Millie dusting and straightening the house with nary a whistle, Evvie eating even less than usual, Jacob staring out the window waiting for something, anything, to happen — the crisis was past and Danny was much better. The doctors took the drain out of his side and stitched him up, and he was free to move about, if cautiously. Clara came in, carrying some gingerbread mice that Evvie had carefully decorated with currants for eyes and wisps of coconut for whiskers, and there he was, sitting up in bed, playing with his old tattered dragon puppet and humming.

"Danny-boy, what's that tune you're humming? It's a feeling-better tune, I hope! Is he finally on the mend, Doctor? He looks much better, really he does."

"Did you ever hear the Chinese proverb?" The doctor smiled. "'A bird does not sing because it has an answer. It sings because it has a song.' But yes, we're not worried any more about the peritonitis. You'll be able to take him home in a few days. That is, if he wants to go home. Or do you prefer it here, Master Daniel?"

"Oh no, I want to go home, please," replied Danny. "Can I?"

"All right, if you insist. But once you get home, you must stay in bed for another week at least. You've been very ill, Danny. No running around or throwing balls or jumping on the furniture until Christmas. Make sure he doesn't exert himself, Mrs. Weiss."

Clara gathered Danny into her arms, careful of his sore scarred belly, and nuzzled into his neck to smell the good boy-smell under the antiseptic. They sat for a long time on the edge of the bed, saying nothing, rocking together as they had when he was still a baby. That rhythm no mother ever loses, with which she comforts even herself; that rhythm so much like the davening of old men in synagogue, praying to a God who never answers.

Silent Night

Chanukah this year was no festival of lights for Clara. Danny was home and doing well, but she was not. An insomniac for the last month, she now got up to check on her son two, three, or even four times a night. Sometimes, in her anxiety to hear his breathing, she inadvertently woke him up. Then she would crawl into his narrow bed, singing quietly until he snuggled into the comfort of her side. His hot little body pressed against hers with the same heedless urgency Ned used to reveal in his sleep, back in the days when he still wanted her. And she lay sleepless beside her youngest child as once she lay sleepless beside her lover.

The memory of those days filled Clara with guilt. Holding Danny night after restless night was a kind of penance, but was it penance enough? Her whole family had suffered for her mad obsession, and now she had to pay the price. Jacob, for example, rarely talked to her anymore. Some part of her oldest son and former confidant had gone underground; he was not so much cold as absent. Clara felt hurt, the more so because she had tried so hard not to trespass on his inner landscape. She remembered from her own childhood what it was like to be denied privacy — to be bullied constantly, forced to explain and define the shifting and indefinable feelings of adolescence. But she missed him. Was she to lose everything because once, just once, she had been a bad mother?

Jacob was clearly making an effort to be kind to his little brother, seating him at the piano and using Danny's chubby index finger to pick out "Twinkle, Twinkle, Little Star" and "London Bridge Is Falling Down." Sometimes he took both his siblings to the library, pulling them all the way there and back in their rusty old bent-axled wagon. He read to them by the hour and even bought them sweets with his own pocket money. This new maturity in her oldest child ought to have pleased Clara, but instead she experienced it as a reproach. Everything around her seemed to whisper that she had failed, that she was no good at anything. That she had *never* been good at anything, and that was why Ned had grown tired of her.

She'd only seen Ned once since he dropped Jacob off after the concert and declined to come in for tea, pleading a prior commitment. That was shortly after Danny's release from hospital. Ned had shown up with a jigsaw puzzle and a chocolate cake, pretending to be an ordinary visitor, but he'd actually come at Clara's request. She'd asked him if he would mind checking up on her stubborn convalescent, who refused to stay in bed and was running around the house as wildly as though he'd never been ill. Unfortunately, Jacob answered the door first and whooped "Dr. Abraham!," with the result that Danny, who had developed quite a fear of doctors while in hospital, refused to accept the puzzle or talk to the man. Instead, he went and sat at the bottom of the stairs with his arms crossed and his eyes fixed sullenly on the hall carpet.

Danny's rejection of his advances elicited an impressive

show of bedside manner from Ned, who had a hidden vein of silliness he rarely indulged. Watching him, Clara couldn't help wondering, once again, why he was so dead set against having children.

"Excuse me, sir. Are you Daniel Weiss?

"Yes."

"You're famous, you know. I hear you fell off a giraffe and cut your tummy on a pineapple."

"No, no, no," said Danny, not realizing at first that it was a joke.

"Oh, pardon me, I forgot. You fell off a pineapple and were bitten by a giraffe."

"You're silly!"

"I'm silly? Not me! I'm not the one who fell out of an apple tree and onto an elephant! Or was it off an elephant's back and into the lion's cage?"

And so on, until her fierce little son relented and pulled up his shirt and allowed himself to be examined. He was proclaimed to be healing beautifully, with a wonderful scar like all the famous soldiers of history. When Danny heard this, he ran off to get a set of toy cavalry, and then he, Jacob, and Ned lay on the carpet comfortably to play battles together until tea was ready. Evvie, who had no interest in war games, busied herself drawing ponies nibbling shiny red apples off low-hanging boughs, drinking from blue rivers full of fish, and carrying beautiful ladies sidesaddle down country lanes.

Clara was meant to be preparing tea, but she couldn't help lingering in the doorway to drink in the scene before her: Ned here, enjoying her children, cheerful and relaxed. This was what she had prayed for all summer. Ned was so good with the boys, so natural. He did different voices for the soldiers, some with French accents, some Italian, some German. He even made convincing whinnying noises for their noble steeds. Very quickly Danny got over his mistrust and scrunched himself up against Ned as close as he could get. Jacob had to remind him to give their guest room to move and then drag his brother off when it was time to come to the table and eat.

But after only a single cup of tea, Ned looked at his watch and said that he had to leave for another appointment. Clara almost cried. Her moment of joy had been an illusion. It was already retreating into that limbo of ghost futures that held their romantic trips abroad, their family holidays by the sea, and their proud attendance, hand in hand, at Jacob's future concerts.

Both the piano and the violin make music by causing strings to vibrate. Perhaps an ancient archer heard the thrumming of the string after his arrow had taken flight. Perhaps he duplicated this phenomenon while idly plucking his bow. Was it because of such inadvertent discoveries that Apollo, god of music, was twinned with his sister Artemis, goddess of the hunt?

Jacob's piano uses more than two hundred strings to play its eighty-eight notes. The long, thick bass strings run singly, the shorter, thinner tenor strings doubly, the slender trebles in threes, like schoolgirls arm-in-arm on a busy street. Piano strings are wire lashed to an iron frame; their tension can be adjusted by a series of pins. It is a laborious job, requiring the services of a professional, so Jacob has to tolerate the increasing dissonance of his instrument in very dry or very cold weather until Clara finally decides they can afford the piano tuner.

By contrast, Ned can, and does, tune his violin often, even obsessively, by himself. Another contrast: the violin has only four strings and yet can attain a seven-octave range. The combined pull of the strings is sixty-five pounds, less than Jacob's weight. By contrast, the stress on the strings of his little upright piano is about sixteen tons. If he ever gets the grand piano of his dreams, it will be closer to twenty-three tons.

Ned felt Jacob pull, he felt the tug of Clara's heartstrings, but resisted. Once he believed himself hunted, he had to run. Paris for Christmas, Vienna in the spring, and by then their plaintive vibrations would have diminished to nothing. He would once more inhabit a lonely but welcoming silence.

The angel surveyed her domain from atop the Christmas tree. Brilliant red and green glass balls and sparkling silver tinsel swung from each branch, vibrating a little with ascending waves of speech and laughter. But something was different, she felt sure. Was the crowd perhaps more subdued than last year, a little more oppressed by a world rumbling towards war? Angels know these things; they can sense the blank spaces in the soul when people surrender to fate.

This boy at the piano, she recognized him, still wearing last year's jacket (though now his wrists shot out of the sleeves, disconcertingly pale and bony). Something else was different about him too. Last year he played rather wildly, giddy with pleasure, this year with sober concentration. His sound was much improved, one might even say heavenly.

But surely he was too young to hold his feelings so sternly in check? He resembled one of those adolescent saints she had always found so dreary, lacking in the gaiety and mischief of the creator of the ostrich and the platypus, whose own rules were inscrutable even to the elect.

Despite her red hair, that woman back there must be his mother. Her pride was clearly visible as rays of light beamed directly at the boy. But it was not an unmixed emotion; unlike the boy (but like too many others in the audience), she couldn't concentrate fully on the music; her mind was elsewhere. She kept looking for someone who wasn't there, and ripples of panic fluttered around her.

The angel decided to close her eyes and just listen. People, God bless them, always got in the way of the music.

The angel wasn't the only one aware of Clara's distraction. Magda Tabori — who had finally confronted Ned about his increasing absence and had been more than a little amused, as well as chagrined, to learn of her rival — was watching Clara too. Something odd was going on there. The woman kept peering anxiously towards the doorway, then fiddling with her hair, which she had cut into a rather unbecoming bob. A shame. Magda always felt sorry for women who capitulated to fashion at the expense of their best features. Nothing would induce her to crop her own luxurious mane, which she kept an age-defying black. Clara's hair had been so distinctive; without it, although she was more fashionable, she looked like everybody else.

Or like anybody else wan and forlorn, anybody else expecting somebody who clearly wasn't there. Probably she was looking for Ned. But didn't she know that he had gone to

Paris? Apparently not, which meant that they weren't seeing each other anymore, or at any rate not very often. Magda wasn't surprised. Ned would never consider a woman like that good enough for him. Clara must be no casual conquest if she could fascinate him for so long, but whatever her gifts were they were not conspicuous and therefore couldn't be a credit to him. Other men wouldn't swoon if he walked by with Clara on his arm, trailing babies and bags and jumpers and books. Women like her smelled too much of the nursery.

That must be why he had called Magda before leaving for Paris, hinting that she might like to go with him and then, when she insisted that she couldn't get away, suggesting an intimate dinner upon his return. Magda knew that Ned would never get tired of *her* because she would never give herself to him completely. That was the trick with men like him, a trick that Clara was doubtless too naive to know or too much in love to practise.

She felt a surge of pity for the woman, and then something rather novel: a rush of maternal concern. She hoped that the boy Jacob had not got dragged into this, for he had talent, genuine talent, and must not become discouraged or confused by the nonsense around him. But perhaps he already had the strength required to concentrate as he must, for his performance of the first three Goldberg variations had been extraordinarily pure, a music purged of all outside influences. The sky after rain, a sandy shore unmarked by a single human footprint. His mother must know that a gift like Jacob's was worth much more than Dr. Edward Abraham's unreliable affections. If she didn't, Magda resolved, she herself would tell her. Yes. They would have a nice little chat, right after the concert.

Magda Tabori sat upright and dazzling in gorgeous furs, the admiring gaze of every man in the room upon her, but Ned wasn't at her side. Clara didn't know whether to be relieved or not. Where on earth could he be? He would miss the austere yet splendid Bach that Jacob had chosen to perform with him in mind. She tried to hold onto the music, to ascend with it above the mess she had made of her life, but she couldn't. She could not escape her body so easily. The morning sickness lasted all day now, and so did her panic.

How could she tell Ned she was pregnant when he didn't even want to see her anymore? (But why didn't he? Did he feel as guilty about Danny's illness as she did? Or did he think she still blamed him for it?) And how on earth had this happened anyway, when they'd taken all the necessary precautions? She knew he would blame her, despite the fact that he had insisted on being in charge of contraception himself, right from the start.

Someone else came on stage to perform the "Meditation" from Massenet's *Thais*. She was young and slender with long golden hair: a fairy-tale princess to whom everything had been promised in advance. On her journey, no path would be too stony, no mountain too steep or cold, no gate locked and barred as they were to Clara, who felt herself always outside, in the rain, alone. Clara looked at this unknown girl with something close to hatred and then found herself weeping and ashamed. Why should she envy strangers, knowing nothing of their real lives beyond this tranced moment of music? Who, after all, knew anything about her: her loneliness, her losses, and her terrible isolation? And of those who knew, who could begin to feel what she felt?

The music was unbearably sweet and sad. All that soaring

aspiration, all those faltering steps back down to earth were making her cry, and Jacob was starting to look embarrassed. She must get back in control, quickly.

"What do you think, Jakey? Is this real?" she whispered to her son.

"Is what real?" he whispered back.

"The feelings in this music. The yearning, you know, the sacrifice."

"Well, she has a nice light touch. And the violin's tuned properly for once. Half the people here can't get their fiddles in tune. But it's just too sentimental for me. It's what Dr. Abraham calls programme music. You know, music that makes people feel obvious things in an obvious way."

He really was becoming someone different, this boy: colder, more critical, of everybody and everything. Ned's influence, as he was proud to remind her.

She strove to regain his interest and respect in an acceptable way. "Well, it's from a French opera. Maybe you'd be more moved by it if you knew the story."

"Maybe. If I knew the story."

And now the choir was singing of blooming madonnas and blessed babes, miraculous and joyful births. Maybe a miracle would happen for her too, and Ned would want his child, and her with it. She would tell him, she would go to his office and find him tomorrow, or if not tomorrow, very soon. And then she would not be alone anymore.

Clara braced herself on the top step, adjusting her hat. She'd never been to Ned's flat before, a fact that now struck her as painfully indicative of everything that had gone wrong. How he'd been willing to see her as Jacob's mother, as a patient, even as a mistress, but not as an equal or a friend. And she'd been so submissive, so grateful for his attention that she'd let him relegate her to below-stairs status, as though he weren't as lucky to have found her as she was to find him. As though he weren't the one who arranged their liaisons and couldn't go more than a fortnight without seeing her. As though he didn't fall asleep peacefully on her breast like a little child.

She knocked and waited, having worked herself into a state of fierce indignation (or having persuaded herself that she must convey indignation rather than despair or the interview would surely fail). But instead of Ned, a very thin, bent old woman with the same startling black eyes opened the door.

"Yes?" she inquired, with a slight Yiddish intonation.

"Is Dr. Abraham in?" Clara tried to keep the quaver of panic out of her voice. Of course she'd known he lived with his mother, but she'd come over in such a rush she hadn't worried about meeting her.

"No, he won't. He won't be back from Paris until tomorrow. At any rate, his office is downstairs. This is his home." The woman, clearly annoyed, assumed that Clara was a pushy patient.

"Oh, yes, I realize that. But this isn't a medical matter," Clara said defensively, without thinking.

"Really? Then what do you want?"

"My name is Clara Weiss. Perhaps Dr. Abraham has spoken of my son Jacob? They played a concert together, a Mozart sonata, last spring."

"Oh, of course! Neddie is so fond of your son. The boy's a natural musician, he says, just like he was at that age." A warm smile transfigured the stiff features of the old woman, and Clara could see how beautiful she must have been as a girl, before joy was chastened from her face. "Come in, come in, my dear. You're soaking wet."

"No, really, I was just passing by. But would you be kind enough to tell Dr. Abraham I called?"

"Only if you have a cup of tea with me first. You mustn't say no, I have so few visitors these days. What it is to grow old — you young people just don't understand."

Thus it was that Clara found herself in Ned's flat for the first time. In spite of herself, she was curious. His coat was gone, but an elegant paisley scarf and a grey fedora still hung on the coat stand. She resisted an overwhelming urge to bury her face in his clothes and forced herself to look around the oak-panelled entry hall, a rigid smile on her face.

At eye level along the opposite wall was a row of sepia photographs: men with long beards, women whose heads were decorously covered by shawls. Old Russian bubbes and zaydes, just like the images she herself had grown up with. The house smelled faintly of fish, overlaid with the more powerful aroma of furniture polish; the wood panelling glowed and the black and white diamond-shaped floor tiles were spotless. Someone clattered in the kitchen. Of course they would have hired help.

"Please make yourself comfortable and I'll ask Ivy to put on the kettle."

Mrs. Abraham shuffled off, favouring an arthritic left hip, leaving Clara perched on the edge of a dark, overstuffed sofa in a dark, overstuffed room. There was no sign of Ned here; there was nothing but the conventional artifacts of his mother's generation. A brass samovar gleamed on a corner table, every seat back was covered with hand-crocheted anti-macassars and needlework pillows, and there were plants everywhere. Ferns, aspidistras, and philodendrons, indestructible shiny plants that salted the air with their green breath. Plants with sharp teeth and rigid spines: an impenetrable jungle. She would never be able to talk to Ned in this house.

But for now she was trapped, at least until after tea. What could she do? What possible excuse could she give for being here? She would have to say she needed advice about Jacob, something to do with his music perhaps, and ask the old lady to have Ned call her at his leisure; she would say she had been in the neighbourhood by chance and that her visit was impulsive. She would have to be very discreet, drink tea politely, and leave without betraying the least hint of her real predicament.

Had Magda Tabori ever been here? Magda, who would feel comfortable anywhere and take charge of any situation, as she had taken charge of Clara herself after the concert, sweeping her off for a nice little chat, while Jacob ate cake under the benevolent supervision of Miss Westerham. Magda, who had told her frankly that she must stop pining after Ned, who was, after all, a "hopeless case," and concentrate instead on cherishing Jacob. Magda, who hugged her close when she began to cry and walked her down the hall into an empty classroom to hear the whole story, her dark, mobile face now stern, now sympathetic, now indignant, now tender. Holding Clara's chapped hand in her soft jewelled one, she wiped away Clara's tears with a lacy handkerchief — real lace, from Belgium, fine as a spider's web; Clara protested at first and refused to dirty it. Tall Magda, who made Clara feel deliciously childlike and who treated her as Clara had always wished her own mother and sister might have, without interrupting or judging or comparing her situation to their own, without belittling or blaming.

It had been extraordinary. The woman of whom she was most afraid, the woman she considered her rival, had given her the most generous support she'd experienced in her life. She had insisted Clara tell Ned the truth immediately because he had a right and a responsibility to be involved. But she had also warned Clara that she must decide what she wanted from him in advance and ask for it, or she was likely to get nothing.

Magda, it seemed, had a very poor opinion of men. Clearly, she must be unhappy in her marriage; for all her fame, she had never been loved as Clara had, and that made her bitter. It also made her blind. She was oblivious to the sweetness in Ned, a hidden boyish sweetness, clandestine as the delicate skin under his clenched jaw that Clara loved to kiss. So here she was, buoyed up by Magda's unhesitating resolve, confronting not Ned but his mother. How odd it was to find herself becoming friendly with Ned's other women. Or perhaps not odd, given that she was pregnant with his child. She already knew so much about his family, and births, like deaths, made families even of enemies.

Her heart lifted a little as Ivy, a solid, stone-faced woman in an incongruously gay apron, all scarlet roses and snaking vines and brilliant yellow tulips, set down a gleaming silver tea service and a plate of shortbread biscuits, and Mrs. Abraham poured them each a cup. Here were flowers; here was food. Possibly her life was about to change for the better, despite everything. It was always possible.

They had finished their tea, and Clara was leafing through a slim album of family photographs with more interest than she let on. Here was Mrs. Abraham as a young mother newly arrived in Leeds: beautiful, frail, clutching her tightly swaddled baby and staring apprehensively at the camera. Here was Mr. Abraham, dashing in a moustache and long black cape, looking extremely pleased with himself. And here was solemn little Ned, in black velvet knickers and white stockings, clutching a full-size violin. An older girl with long fair plaits sat on a piano bench next to him, laughing. This must be his big sister, Alta, of whom he spoke with such affection.

Her hand inadvertently caressed the photograph. He was so small and so determined. In a way, he hadn't changed all that much. She wondered what he'd see if he examined her childhood photographs, a confident girl minding her niece and nephews or a lonely one dreaming over her sketchpad?

"Neddie was such a musical child, humming away while he did his school work or drew pictures, even while eating." Mrs. Abraham's voice broke into her reverie. "He got that from his father, from Chaim. That man sang like an angel and had a wonderful ear for languages. We'd only been in England a year before he fit right in. No one could have guessed he came from Russia as an adult. Me, as you can tell, I'm a different sort."

"Oh no, your English is faultless, really," Clara reassured her.

"But I could never pronounce things properly. I'll be a foreigner until the day I die."

"Does it matter to you?"

"Sometimes. It mattered a lot to Ned. He always wanted so much to fit in. You know, to be a real *English* boy. He was so embarrassed when I drank tea in the Russian manner. I used to love to do that, to hold a sugar cube between my teeth and drink the tea through it. Or even better, a spoonful of jam."

"My father-in-law does that too. He loves apricot."

"Ah, apricot jam is so sweet. Also raspberry is very good."

They sipped their tea appreciatively together for a moment before the old lady continued her train of thought.

"I stopped drinking tea Russian-style for Neddie. And I was careful with my English. He was so ashamed of my bad grammar, he would bring his books home from school and make me practice too. But the one thing I could give him was the right clothes. I was good with a needle, so my children always looked smart."

"Yes, he told me you supported the family by sewing."

"He said that? Well, it wasn't just me in the beginning. His papa had lots of different jobs and always managed to bring in something. Also he was very clever at making investments in real estate."

"Real estate! Not a typical venture for an anarchist, surely?"

"Oh, Chaim was full of contradictions. No one could understand that man. Maybe that was why the ladies admired him so much. But after he left I really did have to support the family by myself."

"That must have been hard."

Mrs. Abraham put down her cup thoughtfully. She shook her head.

"Yes and no. The hardest thing about it was the shame. At first when Chaim left, it was a relief. No more arguments about politics or money, no more fuss about cooking things the way his mama had. No kvetching about everything from Mr. Know-it-all. For the first time in my life, I had a quiet home."

She stood up, walked a couple of paces away, and examined the silvery fronds of a fern. Then, with a sigh, she sat down again, as heavily as such a skeletal old lady could.

"But then I realized that my neighbours blamed me. Me! They said that I had driven my man away by being too cold. That Chaim, he charmed everyone with all that phoney Russian passion. No one knew how impossible he was to live with."

Here she paused for a moment, but when Clara failed to respond, disconcerted by her candour, Mrs. Abraham resumed.

"Ach, they had always been jealous of me. I was surrounded by a bunch of ignorant peasants and yentas, women who never read anything but a recipe book or a Yiddish paper full of scandal. Let me tell you, to be an agunah, an abandoned wife, in that community, was a fate worse than death."

"But surely there were lots of others in your situation?" Clara asked, remembering Ned's stories about all the men from Leeds who went back to fight the revolution.

"Yes and no. Some wives went along from the beginning and some went later, when they were sent for. Some husbands, of course, came back. But mine, he never even wrote us a letter. And everybody knew he was gone for good. Everybody knew." She flung out both her arms as though pushing away the whole unsympathetic crowd. "Still, I could never marry again" — her right hand, clawed with arthritis, went briefly to a gold watch pinned to the bodice of her dress — "though there were good men who would have been happy to have me."

"Oh, I'm so sorry," said Clara. Did Ned know this part of his mother's history? Somehow she doubted it.

"You know, you're lucky your husband actually died. At least you can remarry. You won't have to be alone forever."

"But Mrs. Abraham, surely you're not alone. You have

Ned," said Clara, trying to maintain her composure despite feeling as though she had been slapped. The old lady was not as gentle as she looked.

"Do I? Ned's a good boy, he does his best, but no one has Ned, not even me."

"What do you mean?" asked Clara.

Mrs. Abraham noticed the hesitation in Clara's voice and looked at her brightly, her head cocked to one side like a raven's, her eyes so black the iris was indistinguishable from the pupil. Ned's eyes: dark mirrors, giving back nothing but Clara's own fraught reflection.

"Azoi. You're in love with him, aren't you. Well, you're not the first, and you probably won't be the last. But you see, that's exactly why my son lives with me, to save him from the women. He pretends he's doing his duty, taking care of his poor mother, but really, it's the opposite. He uses me as an excuse to avoid them."

Clara stood up suddenly, nearly knocking her teacup to the floor. This meeting had gone terribly wrong, and Ned would be so cross that she'd talked to his mother without asking. He would see it as spying.

"I'm sorry if I upset you, Mrs. Weiss. When you're my age you just can't be bothered to pretend anymore. It's easier to tell the truth, nu? Everyone finds it out in the end anyway, no matter what you say."

"I suppose so. Really, I don't know. I'm sorry . . . I must go now," Clara replied. She was babbling like an idiot. She *was* an idiot. What on earth had made her think she could just drop in and find Ned alone? She ought to have called him at work and arranged to see him privately. Clearly she was losing her mind.

"But you seem like a very nice person, the kind I wish my son *would* marry," Mrs. Abraham went on, unperturbed. "In fact, you remind me of my daughter, Alta. Fair, just like all Chaim's side of the family. We used to joke about it and call them the White Russians."

Clara stopped. She must say something; it was absurd to stand here like a little girl who'd been punished. She took a deep breath and summoned as much dignity as she could with one arm fumbling in a coat sleeve and the other clutching her battered old purse and tatty umbrella.

"Mrs. Abraham, you should not say such things to me. You know how private Ned . . . I mean Dr. Abraham . . . is."

"Private? Yes. But I like that. Other people — they're too noisy. Even when they don't say anything, they just sit there needing, wanting, taking up space. There's never enough air when there are other people around. Especially children. They're the worst. Well, I'm sure you know what I mean, since you're a mother."

"No, actually, I don't know what you mean. Anyway Ned's not like that, he's kind. You should see how patient he is with my son, Jacob. How could he be a good doctor if he resented people the way you say he does? He gives so much to everyone all the time. I feel sorry for you, Mrs. Abraham. Your life has obviously been difficult, and you have lots of reasons to be bitter. But please don't assume Ned's the same as you are. He's not."

Where had she found the strength for that last speech? Did she even believe it? She hardly knew. But she could not let Ned's mother stand there like a malevolent spider, sucking all the hope from her life. Clara's heels clicked emphatically as she turned her back and marched down the hall, across the gleaming black and white diamonds of tile. Black, white, black, white; whether she was right or wrong, chances were excellent she'd never be visiting again.

Whenever the randomness of the world became too oppressive, Ned found himself seeking refuge in the chaconne from Bach's D-minor partita. He relished the discipline of baroque music, finding it as symmetrical and restorative as a herb garden: a maze demanding unswerving attention and rewarding those who negotiated its twists and turns with a deeply gratifying sense of order. How odd that baroque once meant wild and irregular. One century's caprice so soon becomes another's convention.

But now it seemed things were too broken to be mended by a single session of Bach. Even his mother knew it. Though she rarely intruded — as much to protect her own seclusion as his — today she stood in the doorway, watching. Ned felt her presence but ignored her, although he knew that eventually she would have to say something and he would have to listen.

She finally spoke, her voice dry and almost inflectionless. "There's an old Russian proverb. A wife is not an instrument you can hang on the wall when you're tired of playing on it."

"What wife? What on earth are you talking about, Mama?"

"That Clara. The redhead. The one with the boy. She came here yesterday, looking for you."

"I know. She left a note in the letterbox."

"She's in love with you, you know."

"Love! Oh, really? And what would you know about love, Mrs. Who-knows-where-Chaim-is Abramowicz?" he said, accompanying this salutation by a brief dissonance on the strings. He must not let her disturb his composure. He must not.

She looked at him for a moment. Maybe she deserved his disdain. But then again, maybe she did not. Who could tell? Who could ever know how much her own life shaped, or mis-shaped, the lives of others?

"Don't be a fool, Neddie, or you'll end up all alone like me one day," the old lady said. But when he turned his back on her, she melted into the shadows.

Although his heart was beating faster than he liked, insisting that its story be told, Ned disregarded it. He tried to let his mother's words float past weightlessly, without body or echo — simply noise, like the cars in the street, the rain hitting the windows harder now, almost sleet, the jaws of winter closing in with the early dark.

How he hated this time of year. Ned's family had celebrated neither Chanukah nor Christmas because the revelry around them always seemed so false and contrived. Most revelry did, really; what did any of it matter, birthdays or anniversaries? What was the point of celebrating because the calendar told you to? People must find their own meanings through their own actions, not feel things according to schedule. His mother had taught him that. And if, in her dotage, she intended to join the mundane chorus, well, he'd just have to shut her out too.

What was going on with these women? Clara, Magda, and now Mama all nipping at his heels like the hounds after Actaeon. He still couldn't believe that Clara had confided in Magda, of all people, before even telling *him* she was pregnant. And now Magda was squawking away at him about his responsibility. Who could have imagined she'd have such a conventional streak in her? And Clara, Clara visiting his mother without his permission. This was as much of a betrayal as the pregnancy itself. Why keep the affair secret, as he had thought she wished, and then broadcast its disastrous results? It didn't make sense coming from a faithful daughter of Israel, so maybe all that tremulous respectability had been an act, maybe she had connived at this all along. She must have got pregnant deliberately, intending to trap him. How could he have been such a fool as to trust a widow?

Ned concentrated. He stilled his whirling thoughts, the arrhythmia of which had already begun to affect his playing. His eyes bored into the score and shut out the room. He must focus on nothing else if the music were to expand around him and inside him so there was room only for Bach's patterns, the fine bridges he made over everyone else's turbulence. As always, music was a refuge from the chaos of existence. The only reliable sanctuary. The only thing in his life that had always made sense.

He resolved not to be compelled by circumstance; he would not dignify this absurd situation by calling it fate. He was a free man still, and to relinquish that freedom would be to destroy the meaning of his life. He would solve this problem once and for all, then go to Vienna as he'd planned. And when he came back, the whole thing would have blown over — a wrong note, a bungled passage — and he could resume playing as he had to, cleanly and properly, without ornament or distraction.

Fugue

It was the symmetry that persuaded her. She'd already lost the two between Jacob and Evvie, each at exactly this stage of development. So this would make it three: three babies sacrificed to guarantee the safety of the three she'd been allowed to keep. Her doctor had called the miscarriages "spontaneous abortions," and as Ned had pointed out, there was no assurance that this one would make it safely to its due date no matter what they did. At the moment it was just a blind fish, a wriggling, unthinking thing. No flicker of God's image in any of its features.

Ned had been calm and persuasive, professional, quite sure this was the right thing for them. And his confidence made it easy for Clara to give in to her own selfishness.

Did she want this baby?

No, not at all.

Did she want Ned?

Yes, desperately.

Would getting rid of the one get back the other?

That seemed to be the bargain. After all, Ned kept saying they'd been happy until now. What else could he mean but that things would have continued had the pregnancy not got in the way? He had been so sweet and sympathetic, holding her hand, wiping away her tears with a large snowy handkerchief. Freshly ironed, it smelled of lavender, and his monogram was embroidered in beautiful curly script in one corner. He said she could keep it, he had loads, he bought them by the dozen in Paris.

In retrospect, it was odd how little he'd said about his own feelings. But at the time, he'd appeared preoccupied with how she felt, and she'd been so grateful for his undivided attention that she didn't recognize his reticence. He asked if she was prepared to resume the hard work of mothering an infant, especially now, when she was so worn out from Danny's illness. He wondered whether she was really willing to abandon the prospect of painting, travel and time for herself — all those things she'd given up for the other children that seemed finally within reach. And he seemed just as concerned as she was at the effect her pregnancy would have on the other children, especially Jacob.

Clara knew very well the kind of scandal that would follow the birth of an out-of-wedlock child to someone like her, and she couldn't bear to think of how it would affect her oldest son, who was at such a vulnerable age. That is, if Ned wouldn't marry her. If only Ned would marry her, life could go on as it was meant to. But he eliminated that option immediately. When she timidly broached the subject, he levelled his dark eyes at her and replied, "Surely you wouldn't want to be forced into marriage by an unwanted pregnancy? I've always thought marriage was, well, sacred. A mitzvah. And that when I married it would be freely, out of pure love. And you, Clara, you and Jacob, you've both taught me so much about love."

Even he, who never cried, was crying by then. Moved into

a realm beyond concern with social expectations or moral imperatives, beyond the customs of her people, beyond even her own beliefs, moved into pure wonder at *him* being so moved, she would have agreed to anything. But still she knew she could love this child if Ned wanted it, and she was sure he could love it too, if he let himself. Oh, why wouldn't he let himself? Must this pregnancy be seen as random, or could it not be, somehow, a little nudge towards future joy? Could it not be celebrated?

Later, she could not remember how much of this she said out loud to Ned and how much she was just thinking as he calmly but firmly rebutted all her tentative arguments. It was as though there were two of her. Maybe there had been two of her ever since she met him, one glad to be relieved of responsibility by letting him make all the decisions, the other afraid to ask for what she knew she wouldn't get — or perhaps, more obscurely, more terribly, afraid to ask in case she got it.

"We did not plan this pregnancy, so we must not be held hostage to it. We are modern people, and there are safe modern means to resolve this situation. Let's use them and then get back to our real lives. I promise I'll take excellent care of you, Clara. You'll be fine." He was holding her hand, stroking her cheek, speaking so softly. Coming to her rescue, as he had in the street when she cut her leg, and then again in the hospital when Danny was sick. This was the third time. In that realm, where two spirits hugged against the cold, she agreed. Translating, she said it was the symmetry that persuaded her.

So they did it, quickly and efficiently. Scrubbed and gowned, pragmatic comrades-in-arms, they made the helpless creature into something at once malign and pathetic, a serious threat that was simultaneously nothing more than an unfortunate accident. She was never actually sure which it was, then or later.

Jacob had discovered something amazing. Here he was, trying to teach Danny to play the piano, and all along it was Evvie who had the talent. Exceptional talent, so exceptional that Jacob was a little uncomfortable, though he hardly dared confront his own thoughts. He'd always been the gifted one and she just an ordinary girl, with stringy hair and a runny nose, a solemn and comical little thing. Could it really be that music lived in her so easily? And would it now abandon him?

But why hadn't they noticed before? It was true that his sister always listened intently as he practised and made sensible comments about his performance, true that she always sang in key, though never very robustly. But who would have guessed that, by watching him give basic instruction to Danny, she could pick up the rudiments of the keyboard quickly enough to play almost anything by ear?

Jacob brought Evvie to his lesson with Miss Westerham, and the teacher confirmed what he already suspected. His sister had perfect pitch and unusual musical ability. Oddly enough, Evvie herself was not impressed by her own gifts; if anything, she was embarrassed. Miss Westerham was willing to teach her for free, given their mother's financial situation and her existing commitment to Jacob, but Evvie wasn't even sure she wanted to accept the offer.

"Don't be such a ninny! Don't you like playing the piano?" Jacob said.

"I like music, but I don't like playing it for other people. Everyone's so bossy, especially Miss Westerham. Her voice gives me a headache."

Jacob had to laugh at this. "I know what you mean. Well, if she's not the right teacher for you, I could try to find someone . . . quieter."

"You could teach me, Jakey."

"I don't think that's a good idea. You'd get bad habits from me, or I'd lose my temper and you'd cry, and then we'd both feel rotten. No, Evvie, you definitely need a real teacher, someone outside the family."

"Anyhow, I'm not sure I want to play the piano. I can't reach all the notes. I think I'd like violin better. It's more cuddly."

"Cuddly?" Jacob laughed again. "I don't know if Dr. Abraham would agree with you about that. The violin's jolly hard, you know. I mean, the notes sound so horrible and screechy if you don't get them just right."

"I'd get them right."

"You know what? I believe you would. So let's go ask Mum to call Dr. Abraham about a good teacher. I'm sure he'll know somebody for you. He knows everyone!"

Luckily Miss Westerham also knew everyone, so Clara didn't have to call Ned to find the perfect teacher for Evvie. Mr. Leopold was a Polish refugee, an old man with military shoulders but a very tranquil manner. He came to the house once a week, bringing pastry and compliments and Old World charm. His gentle presence reassured Clara that the chaos of the last few months was finally over.

The worst had been right after. It had been much worse

than the other times, with heavy bleeding and cramps almost as bad as labour. She had covered her bed with towels, which she later washed surreptitiously, hiding them from Millie. She bit into her pillow to stifle the groans tearing out of her, harsh animal sounds oddly resembling the growls of pleasure that resonated through her stolen hours with Ned, as though to insist on the inescapable relationship of cause and effect.

The old migraine excuse kept the family out of her darkened bedroom for a couple of days only. Then for two more weeks Alice kept popping in unannounced, alternately straightening Clara's blankets and scolding her for inertia. Danny curled up beside her clutching a toy soldier in each hand, narrating imaginary battles; Evvie sat cross-legged on the end of her bed, dreamily sucking her thumb; Jacob brought her endless cups of tea. But still Clara lay there, overcome by lassitude one minute and anguish the next. For though Ned telephoned a couple of times and sent her a beautiful arrangement of yellow lilies, orange chrysanthemums and silky ferns — perfectly calculated to go with the colours of her house, obviously expensive as well as thoughtfully chosen — she knew in her heart that he wasn't coming back to her, that he'd already left her before he even knew she was pregnant, and that she'd been lying to herself all along. She'd never had a future with Ned, she saw that now. All they'd ever had was the present. A present so fierce it burned itself up and left nothing behind but the sheen of sweat on their skins.

"What's going on, Mum? You have to tell us. Do you have cancer too? Are we going to have to live with Aunt Alice from now on?" Jacob's voice cracked a little, as it was starting to do, and his skinny boy's body seemed to hum with fear and indignation. Stricken, Clara noticed that he'd even begun to bite his nails again, a habit he'd finally broken last year.

"Oh no, my darling, no! I'm sorry you've been so worried. I . . . I have been sick, yes, but I'm much better now. I've just needed a lot of rest, that's all. Look, why don't you go ask Millie to make us a nice cup of tea while I get washed and dressed? Jacob, sometimes even adults have problems. You'll understand better when you grow up."

"I'm grown up already, Mum. You just haven't noticed."

"You're not as grown up as you think you are, my lad!" She laughed for the first time in weeks. The reality of her life with its intimate muddle of feelings flooded into her, and the single flame that had consumed her flickered and grew less. It would not go out entirely, not ever, but become one of many griefs at the periphery of thought. Losing Ned was not the only truth of her existence, as it had seemed until Jacob stood there in righteous fury, blazing and beautiful and hers. Needing a haircut.

Clara never went back to bed; the helplessness had gone. She might have made a mess of her life but it was *her* life, and she had to take charge of it. So she got up and bathed and dressed herself smartly; she even put on a spray of perfume and a dab of lipstick, shockingly bright against the pallor of her skin. And after a couple of quiet days on the sofa, reading to Danny and Evvie, she decided it was time to clean the house. It needed a cleaning; more than that, it needed a ritual purification. Everywhere she looked she saw signs of creeping decay: chipped baseboards, dirty windowpanes, peeling wallpaper. The kitchen faucet needed a new washer, the front door wanted a new coat of paint. For too long she'd let everything go, lost in silly adolescent fantasies of love and freedom.

Each day Clara and Millie tackled another project, including some that they'd never attempted before. They beat carpets, washed all the windows with vinegar and water, scrubbed fingerprints off walls, polished the silver, hung new wallpaper in the entry hall, and turned out every closet and drawer. They took down the light fixtures to empty them of dust and dead flies, to Danny's horror and delight. They dismantled the dining room chandelier and washed each prism carefully. Even the heavy mahogany table and chairs she'd inherited from her parents and never really liked, hulking there like the ghost of a thousand tedious family dinners, shone with new life and smelled wonderfully of lemon oil. Spring was coming, Clara declared, throwing open the windows and letting the sun and air stream in. It was time to put things right.

"My mother used to spring clean like a fury as well," said Millie. "It's grand to have a good turn-out once a year. You always find things you didn't remember you had, like that blue cardigan I knitted for Evvie we thought was lost. The one with the yellow duck on the pocket."

"It's too small anyway, Millie. It pulls under my arms."

"Then give it to your brother. He likes blue too, don't you, Danny?"

"Not that kind of blue," he wailed. "It's for girls!"

"Nonsense, Danny," said Clara, continuing to fold discarded garments into a box. It was amazing how much work there was to do around the house once you got going. Really, it could absorb every minute of every day if you let it.

"Blue is for everyone," she went on. "The sky is blue. Is the sky just for girls? The sea is blue. Is the sea just for girls?"

"But I don't want Evvie's clothes, I want Jacob's. I'm a big boy now, Mama."

"Of course you are, my love. But big boys wear cardigans

too, don't they? Anyhow, let's wait till we've finished cleaning and see what's what. There may be some other things you like better. Then, what neither of you want we can put in this box for the orphanage."

"What's an orphanage?" asked Danny.

"Where children live whose parents are dead, silly. Don't you know anything?" Evvie replied.

She was twirling around in her mother's old slip and a hat with a dotted veil, feeling very glamorous and grown-up. She would wear the hat to her first concert, she thought, with the veil down, and everyone would wonder who that mysterious beautiful lady was and fall madly in love with her when she started to play. She might keep the veil down for the whole concert and then escape into the night on a white horse, with no one ever seeing her face. She might.

"Don't call him silly, Evvie. You know what Zayde always says, you'll never learn anything if you're afraid to ask questions."

"Can I ask something else then, Mama?"

"What is it, Danny?"

"My papa's dead, so am I an orphan?"

"Poor wee thing," cried Millie, gathering him up in her arms.

"No, pet, you've still got me, haven't you?" Clara replied, tickling him. "And aunts and uncles, and lots of cousins, and a grandfather who's coming to tea. You'll never need to worry about going to an orphanage. We'll take care of you forever and ever."

Zayde held Jacob's hand a little too tightly as they walked over to the Hammersmith synagogue, an unassuming red brick building looking more like a school than a place of worship. It advertised its presence only by the carving of the Ten Commandments set up over its entrance and the Jewish stars engraved on its staircases and shining from its stained glass windows. The old man usually didn't frequent the "Englischer shul," preferring his neighbourhood synagogue full of other Yiddish speakers, but lately he'd started staying over Friday nights so he could take Jacob to morning services. Sometimes the rest of the family came as well, but mostly not. Danny found it too hard to sit still and Clara, in the thick press of other people's families, missed her own too much. Besides, she said, it was nice for Jacob and Zayde to have time alone together, especially before his bar mitzvah.

And it *was* nice for Jacob to be able to walk into shul with his grandfather. It was nice to sit next to him, wrapped in the comforting folds of the old man's prayer shawl and playing with its fringe, separating the tangled threads and then braiding them together during particularly tedious passages of text. A musty but not unpleasant smell came from Zayde's tallis. Jacob thought it must be the smell of time.

Zayde too smelled of time. Maybe it was just that Jacob was getting taller, but his grandfather seemed to be shrinking, his shoulders hunched, his head peering up from his chest like a turtle's from its shell. He kept his sparse grey hair short and his beard neatly trimmed; he was not one of those pee-stained, decrepit old men who inspired as much pity as revulsion. Far from it. His eyes and his mind were as bright as ever. But his body was failing and, with it, some of his courage.

So he held Jacob's hand too tightly. He fussed over how thin Evvie was, bringing her fancy biscuits, strudel, and boxes of chocolates, much to Clara's disapproval. He worried about

Danny's health too, challenging him constantly to show that he had recovered from his illness. How fast can you run? How high can you jump? Just look how strong the boy is, a regular Hercules.

"Look, Zayde, I can pick up Evvie, and she's going to be six."

"Soon you'll be able to pick me up too. I won't even have to walk to the park anymore. I'll just ride there like a prince."

"Don't encourage him, please. Put your sister down at once, Daniel, before someone gets hurt."

"Your mother's right, tateleh. Now come over here and sit on Zayde's lap, and I'll read you a story."

He was spending more and more time at their house, playing checkers with the children, helping Jacob with his Hebrew, sitting quietly in a corner with a book, shaking his head and muttering to himself. And it had finally come out: he was afraid to be home alone, for Mosley's thugs were on the march in the East End, yelling, "Kill the Jews! They've got your jobs." His own windows had been broken twice now, and three times his walls had been smeared with hostile words.

He hadn't told Clara at first. Since she'd already suffered through Danny's illness and her own, he wanted to protect her. But he had told Jacob, on one of their Saturday morning walks to shul.

"You're the man of the house now, Yakov. After your bar mitzvah you'll be a man officially. So you have to understand these things. There is danger in the world for us."

"Everyone knows about the Nazis, Zayde. But they're crazy!"

"Crazy yes, but strong. Too strong. Who will protect us from them?"

"England will."

"From your mouth to God's ears."

"They're not going to get us, Zayde, stop worrying. We survived Pharaoh. We survived Haman. We even survived the Inquisition. The rabbi said that's how we know the Israelites are the chosen people, because none of the other nations from those days are still around. There's no more Assyrians or Sumerians or Babylonians. But *we're* still here."

The old man smiled and hugged his grandson tight. It consoled him to hear Jacob speak of their small, embattled tribe as "we," as "the Israelites," as though they had some status with the outside world. Well, perhaps this generation would succeed where earlier ones had not, making a place for themselves in spite of those who sought their destruction. But he doubted he'd live long enough to see it.

Clara was concerned about the change in Zayde. Trying to understand what was going on, feeling impelled to reassure her father-in-law, she returned to her newspapers. But there was no reassurance to be had there; things really were as bad as he said. Hitler invaded the Rhineland, unopposed as usual, and the pogroms in Poland were as terrible as those from which Zayde had fled fifty years ago. She started to have nightmares, nightmares she suspected were somehow transmitted from him. Children falling from high windows, falling and falling but never hitting the ground. Children bursting into flame, their clothes a grotesque halo. Children calling vainly for their mothers as soldiers marched them off into the dark. The tramp of boots — left, right, left, right — merged with the thudding of her heart. And then she woke, her nightgown dank with sweat.

Clara started thinking of moving to Canada again. After everything she'd been through, it might be nice to live somewhere else, far away. She could join Arthur, who had invited her to come to Montreal many times. But of course her own children would never want to live in another country, and what would Zayde do if they left him here all alone? He would be a lost soul. She decided instead that the old man must move in with them immediately. They would let the flat over the store. It was her turn to take care of him, and to be honest, she needed the security of another adult in the house with her. Now that she had finally admitted to herself that it wasn't going to be Dr. Edward Abraham, violinist and cad, seducer of mothers, killer of babies, it might as well be her sweet-natured father-in-law.

Zayde capitulated with only a mild show of protest and moved into Jacob's room with one trunk, a picture of his late wife, and four boxes of books. So little to show for so long a life. To keep out of everyone's way, he spent most of his time reading or going for walks in the neighbourhood. He did all the grocery shopping, which was definitely a help, and he loved to play with Evvie and Danny. The house felt a little more crowded, and deep down Clara knew she was panicking, but she was determined not to be engulfed by the whirlpool of despair. Her life had suddenly become very simple. She would just concentrate on getting through each day. One foot in front of the other, breakfast, lunch, and supper, school days and holidays. She had done this before, after Leonard died. She could do it again.

And she was managing, really she was, she had her feelings well under control, she was soldiering on, until the day the letter arrived. The letter with the fancy crest on it addressed to Mr. Jacob Weiss, Esquire. She put it aside, having no idea what it could possibly be, until Jacob came in and saw the envelope lying on the hall table.

Ripping it open eagerly, he gave a little whoop and cried, "I got it! I got it!"

"Got what? What's this about, Jacob?"

"I got a music scholarship, Mum. Isn't that amazing?"

"Why didn't Miss Westerham tell me you were applying for one?"

"Because she didn't know about it."

"What do you mean? How on earth could you apply for a music scholarship all by yourself?" She studied the letter. It congratulated Jacob on his talent and offered him admission to Dulwich College, with a subsidy covering most of his tuition for the next school year.

"Well, Dr. Abraham helped me. It was supposed to be a surprise. Dr. Abraham said we'd better not say anything to you in case I didn't get it because then there would be a lot of fuss for nothing."

Clara was stunned. What was going on? Hadn't Ned left them? Left her? She took a deep breath and tried to respond calmly. "Slow down please. What does Dr. Abraham have to do with this scholarship? Was applying for it his idea?"

"Sort of. But I wanted to. He took me there and —"

"He took you to Dulwich College? When did all this happen?"

"Oh, one day in October when you were at the hospital with Danny. But don't blame Millie, I told her I was at Nathaniel's house, she didn't know. We thought you'd be pleased, Mum, honestly. It's so nice there, you can't imagine. It's like some kind of medieval town with old buildings, enormous green fields, and lots of trees."

Of course those places were nice, but nice was for rich

boys. For rich goyish boys. The whole idea was outrageous. It was miles and miles away, it would take Jacob at least an hour to get there each day, alone, on the tube. How dare Ned tempt her son in this fashion?

She tried to control her voice, though fury was rising in her gorge.

"Jacob, have you any idea what a school like this one costs?"

"No, not really. But they said they would give me some money. See, it's right here in the letter."

"Yes, I see. *Some* money. That's very nice, really it is. But where is the rest of it supposed to come from?"

"Don't start screaming at me again!"

"What do you mean again? I haven't been screaming at you. Besides, I'm not cross with you, I'm cross with Dr. Abraham. He had no business to interfere in your education without discussing it with me first."

"He's my friend, Mum. He was only trying to help. He knows I hate my school, that I need to go somewhere else. Here everyone picks on me. There I'd be with people like me, people who like music better than football."

Stricken, Clara wrapped her arms around him and kissed his soft cheek, already nearly level with her own. Why hadn't he told her he was unhappy at school? Shouldn't she have realized it without having to be told? Once again, apparently, she had failed as a mother. Maybe Ned was right. She didn't deserve to have a child as wonderful as Jacob.

Still, Jacob was *her* child, not Ned's, whether or not she deserved him. She didn't want to dash Jacob's hopes and deny him a splendid opportunity, but there was no way she would allow herself to be manipulated.

"Oh Jacob, my darling, darling Jacob, if you're unhappy

at your school then of course we'll find you another. But it ought to be close enough that you can walk there. This Dulwich College is dreadfully far away. You'd be gone all day, travelling on your own. And even with the scholarship, wonderful as it is, we can't afford such a fancy place. There are so many extras: uniforms, tube fare, meals . . . I don't see how we could possibly manage."

"Calm down, will you, Mum? It was just an idea, that's all," said Jacob, unexpectedly relieved. He really hadn't been ready to leave home anyway. Not yet.

But the fuss wasn't over. Alice came by Sunday after lunch to take Clara and the children for a drive in the country. They were going to see the new lambs as a special treat for Evvie's birthday, and even Jacob found himself grinning in anticipation. The journey wasn't particularly tedious, except for Danny asking every five minutes how long it would be till they arrived and Evvie yelling at him to be quiet, he was giving her a headache. Alice always had lots of gossip and was quite content to maintain a monologue as long as her sister interjected a suitable comment from time to time to indicate that she was listening. But when they reached the farm and Clara stiffened at the children's delight in the tiny exuberant creatures, then started to cry when Evvie insisted on giving each lamb a special name and a noisy kiss on its unsanitary wet nose, Alice recognized that something was seriously wrong.

So while the farmer's wife was giving the children their tea in the kitchen, she asked Jacob to keep an eye on the little ones and invited Clara to come with her for a walk. They trudged up the hill behind the lambing shed and then sat down on an old stone wall to rest, admiring the view of the valley below. The countryside was so peaceful and green it seemed no violence could disturb it, and yet the farmer had told them he'd had to shoot a fox that very morning for getting into the henhouse. Was any place in the world truly safe? Clara started to cry again.

"What is going on, sweetheart? Why are you so miserable?"

"I can't tell you."

"What do you mean you can't tell me? You're my baby sister. You're all the family I have! We mustn't keep secrets from each other." Alice took the smaller woman's chin in her hands and lifted it to force Clara to meet her eyes.

"'Danny's well now, isn't he? And what about you — are you still sick? Clara, please, please, I beg of you. Tell me what's going on!"

"Oh no, no, nothing like that, thank God! We're all fine," said Clara, immediately feeling guilty that she'd worried her sister, who was so good to them all, a second mother really. She always took advantage of Alice without appreciating her genuine concern. How selfish she was, how hopeless. She disgusted herself.

"Then what is it?"

Clara just sat there shaking her downcast head, unable to speak.

"I know. It's that man, isn't it? That Dr. Abraham. What's he done to you, darling? I never trusted him, not for one minute. I never trust anyone that good looking, especially when he still lives with his mother."

Clara had to laugh at that, though she still refused to raise her head.

"I'm right, aren't I? You think I don't notice these things, but I do. I couldn't believe you really had a migraine for two weeks. My migraines never keep me in bed that long, and they are hell, absolute hell. I know about migraines, Clara, and I know about men."

Clara laughed again, a strangled sound halfway between a snort and a sob.

"You think I'm joking? You think I don't know about men? Listen here, young lady, before I married Sidney I had lots of admirers. Lots! Mama was always frantic with worry about it. You're too young to remember how she would wait up for me in the front room until all hours, knitting away. And my Sidney himself was quite the bon vivant. I'll bet you didn't know that he was engaged to two other girls before me. In those days he was a real catch, rich *and* handsome, God bless his sweet bald head! But he was still living with his mother. That was the problem, his witch of a mother. She made him break off the other engagements, you know. But she couldn't get rid of me so easily."

Alice finally paused for breath. Clara had looked up, enthralled, in spite of herself. Why had she never heard this story before? Or maybe she had never listened to it properly.

Alice put an arm around her sister's shoulders and pulled her close.

"Sidney wanted me, you see, but I made him wait. Marriage or nothing, I insisted. That's the only way with men like that, men who think they can get any girl they want."

At this Clara broke down completely, sobbing on Alice's shoulder.

"I thought so." Alice stroked Clara's head, her pale bare neck. "I knew when you cut your hair off something was wrong. Anyone who really loved you would love your beautiful, beautiful hair. Did it start before I met him at Passover?"

"No," Clara whispered. She had vowed not to speak of the affair to anyone, but since Alice already knew, what difference could a few details make? "Not really. I guess it started that night."

"What do you mean? How?"

"He kissed me in the gazebo."

"Just a kiss?"

"Just a kiss."

"You should have stopped there," Alice said.

"I know that now, believe me. But I was so lonely. And he was so kind to Jacob. I thought . . . I don't know what I thought. That he was a mensch, I guess. That because he loved music he must be a good person."

And somehow she found herself confiding the whole story, from when they made love that first time in Ned's office, to their last meeting, when he performed the abortion. Alice was so upset that Clara had a hard time calming her down enough for them to go back to the children, who were reluctant to leave the farm dog and the cats and the lambs and didn't want to get back in the car. But now that she had finally told someone her secret, Clara was preternaturally calm. She bought a wheel of sheep's milk cheese for Zayde and two skeins of homespun wool for Millie. She kissed Evvie's favourite lamb, Snowflake, goodbye. And she kept the children busy counting things — ponies, churches, bicycles, letterboxes — all the way home, as Alice seethed and muttered, her knuckles white on the steering wheel, refusing to be distracted from her righteous fury at Ned and her grief for the lost child.

When they got there Alice insisted on coming in, ostensibly to carry Danny, who was fast asleep, up to bed. Though Clara pleaded fatigue, her sister insisted that she shouldn't be

alone at a time like this. In her new state of exhausted seren-
ity, Clara gave up protesting. She asked Zayde to read Evvie
a story and put her to bed, told Jacob to finish his lessons,
and went around the house picking up discarded clothes and
tidying things until she could put off a final confrontation
no longer. She found Alice at the kitchen table, reading the
scholarship letter with a puzzled expression on her face.

"What's this, then?" she asked. "Why didn't you tell me
you'd decided to send Jacob to Dulwich College?"

"Because I'm not sending him there."

"Then why did you apply for a scholarship?"

"I didn't. To be honest, I knew nothing about it. It was a
little . . . adventure he went on with Ned."

"What do you mean?"

"Oh, Jacob told Ned he was unhappy at school, so Ned
took him to Dulwich to see if he liked it. Apparently they
have an exceptional music program, and they said they would
give Jakey a scholarship. But even so, it's too expensive for
us, and too far away. I don't want him to travel that much
every day."

Alice stood up so abruptly her chair fell over. Zayde called
from upstairs, "Is anything the matter?" and Alice reassured
him with exaggerated gaiety before muttering to Clara in a
stage whisper, "I can't believe what I'm hearing! What has
that man done to your brain, Clara? You used to be the smart
one in the family. My God — first he seduces you, then he
murders your baby, and you *still* defer to his judgement? He
has no right, no right at all, to make decisions for Jacob."

"I'm sure he meant well, Alice, really. He loves Jacob, I
know he does."

"Is that so? Then why wouldn't he marry you and prove
it by becoming Jacob's father?"

Silent tears poured down Clara's face. Alice felt a little ashamed at making her sister cry again but was glad to have broken through her infuriating reserve. She righted the toppled chair, then turned, shaking the scholarship letter at Clara.

"He thinks he's better than everybody else, Clara, I could see that at Passover. He was looking down on us all, sneering, making high-handed comments, picking at my good dinner as though it wasn't fancy enough for him. I wish I'd poisoned his soup! But we'll find a way to pay him back, don't you worry. I know exactly what to do."

After Alice left, promising Clara that she would handle things, assuring her that it wasn't simply a matter of revenge, which after all was best left to God, but of protecting other women from a known predator, Clara spent a sleepless night. Alice hadn't said anything she hadn't already thought herself, but it was so humiliating to hear it coming from somebody else — especially from her sister, whom she'd always thought of as dull and conventional. But Alice was right, of course. How could she have fallen in love with someone who looked down on her? When had she become so needy that she would accept any degradation just to have a man's arms around her?

Or maybe it wasn't really her fault. After all, as Alice had reminded her, Ned had seduced her when she was weak and frightened, when she was in too much pain from her cut leg to think clearly. Maybe he had intended this all along. He recognized how vulnerable she was and used all his charm to invade her life and steal Jacob away. He'd never really wanted her at all.

He was an evil man; she saw that now. And getting close to him had endangered her whole family. First she'd almost lost Danny because of him, then he'd made her destroy the baby. And his influence had already turned her oldest boy against her. For months now, Jacob had barely spoken to her, barely even tolerated her presence. If she was to get her old Jacob back, Ned must be cast out forever. Alice was right. She had to make sure he would never hurt them — or anyone else — ever again.

So on Monday, Clara let Alice sweep her away to finish the affair once and for all. They drove across town in an uneasy silence to the General Medical Council. Clara peered out the window, guilt and grief driving a wedge between herself and the world beyond the glass. It was grey and wet. From time to time, the sun pulled back its mantle of cloud to peer out suspiciously before withdrawing again. People walked along under the private canopies of their umbrellas; each pedestrian might as well have been alone in this city, with its tall impersonal facades and quick dirty pigeons, its streets full of litter and honking cars, its beggars and bankers. Alone as she was and must remain.

She was tired, so tired that her very bones hurt. If only she could have slept, she might have been prepared for the ordeal ahead of her. It was all happening too fast. But here they were. Alice said, "Get out, dear," and Clara stood meekly by the curb, the wind flicking rain at her face and swirling filthy papers around her feet. She felt nothing, nothing at all. Was it only yesterday she had watched those newborn lambs leaping with pure joy? Would she ever feel joy like that again?

Then Alice took her arm and helped her up the steps, through the heavy front door, into a marble foyer and then down a hall to a large office with an important brass plate on the door. A punctilious secretary showed them to another office where a very tall man with glasses sat behind an enormous oak desk. Alice explained the situation briskly: "This is my sister, Mrs. Clara Weiss, widow, of Brook Green, London. She has been taken advantage of by a member of the medical profession." The tall man stood up with an expression of grave solicitude on his long thin face. Alice explained that her sister had been seduced and then made to endure an abortion before the man raised his hand to stop her. He would need a formal statement from the victim. He would have to ask Clara a series of questions that might be painful to answer, but he assured her of confidentiality, serious investigation, and serious consequences. Alice said that was what they had come for. Clara said nothing.

Then the man pulled two armchairs up to his desk and asked the ladies to be seated. He took out a stack of forms printed on buff paper and placed a green pen on top of them. He opened a fresh bottle of black ink, filled the pen, and blotted the nib on a square of pink blotting paper. Clara watched with a kind of hallucinatory intensity. Everything in the room appeared so vivid, she felt she might cut herself on the edge of the oak desk, on the tweed upholstery of her chair, on the man's large-knuckled, square-nailed hand, which he had offered to her and then withdrew when she failed to shake it.

The man asked if she was ready to begin. She nodded. The roaring in her ears made her feel she might faint at any moment. She concentrated on sitting upright in her chair, her hands clasped firmly on her handbag.

"What is the name of the man of whom are we speaking?"

"Ned . . . Dr. Edward Abraham. His practice is in Hackney."

"Was he your personal physician?"

"No, he wasn't," Clara began, before Alice cut in. "Yes he was, Clara, he was so! The first time he seduced you was when he was treating your cut leg. She's still protecting him, sir, because he played music with her son. But the fact is that he took advantage of her weakness when he was acting in a medical capacity. And he has to be stopped before he does it again."

"Is this true?" the man asked, his magnified gaze drilling into Clara, and she found herself forced to concur. She tried to explain further, painfully aware of how inadequate such a description was to the complexity of her relationship with Ned, but the man said she should keep her answers short and simple. It was Dr. Abraham's behaviour that was in question here, not hers. Still, several times she felt like saying, I'm sorry, I just can't do this, and running out of the room, but then Alice would squeeze her hand or give her a nudge, and she'd carry on.

"Weren't you aware that abortion is against the law in this country?"

"Well, in theory. But he was a doctor, and he said it would be all right."

"So you deferred to his authority?"

"Yes, I suppose so. Although it was my fault too, of course. I should have had the baby, I see that now. But I didn't know what else to do. I've been alone. So alone."

Clara's voice rose to a wail and, ashamed, she buried her face in Alice's mink-covered shoulder. It was exquisitely soft and dark as earth. How she wished she could burrow into it and disappear, like the timid useless thing she was. The clock ticked. The tall man shuffled his papers and cleared his throat. And finally he said, "I have to ask you one more question, madam, though I realize it might be upsetting."

"I'm sorry. I didn't mean to do that. I'm better now. Go on."

"I understand you are a widow."

"Yes. My husband died three years ago. He had stomach cancer."

"Had you and Dr. Abraham plans to marry?"

"No, not explicitly. But I had reason to believe that . . . that he loved me."

"Then why did you abort his child?"

"He didn't want it. He said we needn't be victims of fate, you see, that we were modern. That we could be free to make our own decisions, rather than having them imposed upon us."

"Well then, was this your own decision?"

"I don't know anymore, honestly. I felt at the time that it was what we both wanted. Mostly I wanted to make him happy. To make him stay with me."

"And was he happy?"

"I don't know."

"And did he stay with you?"

"No. No, he didn't."

And still in a daze, she signed the forms in triplicate, and Alice witnessed them and shook the tall man's hand. Then Clara stumbled down the cool marble corridor, clutching her sister's arm, to emerge into dazzling midday sunlight. Alice unbuttoned her coat and gave a huge sigh of relief.

"You did brilliantly, darling. That bastard hasn't got a hope of keeping his licence. Think of all the other women you've saved by putting him out of business. You did a brave thing, my little Clara. I'm so proud of you." And she offered to take Clara out to lunch "to celebrate."

But Clara only whispered, "No, no, I need to get home," and collapsed in the car, eyes closed against the jubilant spring light, ears shut to Alice's incessant chatter. What have I done? she thought. God forgive me, what have I done?

"You look better than I expected, Edward. What have you been doing with yourself?" asked Magda, fitting a slender black Russian cigarette into a golden holder. She was wearing an emerald green dress with a low-cut black satin collar, which emphasized her statuesque figure. Every eye in the place was on her and a murmur of approval had followed her progress across the room. Ned, who'd arrived at the restaurant early and already had a stiff brandy, felt quite giddy with anticipation of the evening ahead.

"Playing truant. Oh, I've had a marvellous time, really. I've been reading, playing music, taking long walks, and seeing old friends. I think there are plenty of opportunities for me here, you know."

"I find that hard to believe. Vienna has changed so much I don't recognize it. People are looking over their shoulders and censoring what they say. Even me, Edward. Everywhere I look I see Nazis, like those brutes at the corner table."

"I'm surprised at you, Magda. Haven't you always boasted that you're at home everywhere?"

"Well, I'm not anymore. The world is getting smaller. I want to go back to Budapest and hide, really I do. I want to tunnel in like a rabbit and wait until the hawks have flown away."

Ned laughed out loud at the image of elegant Magda cowering in the dirt. But she shook her head at him.

"I am serious. Even Stefan is worried now, and he has always been so blasé about everything. He says Hitler is going to march into Austria any day. Vienna is not safe for anyone Jewish. You must go back to England right away, Edward."

She whispered this as though the drunken quartet at the far table could hear them, but her wariness served only to irritate Ned.

"I am *not* crawling back to England, Magda. There's nothing for me there anymore. I've lost my licence and am not allowed to work. A very boring dentist from Norwich is taking over the surgery, and my mother's planning to go live with Alta in Manchester. I even had to sell my beautiful new car. My God, I loved that car!"

"I am so sorry, Edward."

"Well, maybe it's for the best. I felt like an outsider in England anyway, no matter what I did. Music has always been my real home, and there's wonderful music here. When I had a medical career, it was hard to take time off to do the things I really wanted, like climbing the Alps. So now I'm going to climb the Alps."

"But it is not safe for you here."

"I thought your precious Stefan said Herr Hitler was just a puppet."

"Yes, he did. But so did a lot of very knowledgeable people until recently. Hitler was just so silly looking, so vulgar. It seemed impossible that someone like him could become truly powerful, impossible that people would believe his obscene ravings. But as I already said, the world has changed."

Ned laughed: a sharp, ironic expulsion of breath. Hope deflating. This evening would not be what he'd longed for, all perfume and sex and Magda's throaty laughter. Even Magda wasn't laughing anymore.

"We always thought that if the world changed, it would change for the better," he finally said.

She took his hand in hers, raised it to her lips.

"So you do care, after all."

"I have always cared, you know that. You are the problem."

"Me? I'm not the one who's married!"

"No, apparently not."

"What's that supposed to mean?"

"You know very well."

"You sound like my mother. I was *not* married to that woman."

"That woman? Listen to yourself, Edward. You can't even say her name."

"Clara, then. See? I can say her name. I was not married to Clara, damn bloody Clara. We were just intimate, we did what men and women always do. What you and I have done. The only difference was that this time there were unfortunate consequences. As it turns out, they were far worse for me than for her. She still has her home, her family, her reputation . . . Why did she do it, Magda? I lost everything. *Everything*."

"You think Clara did not lose a great deal? Edward, she was in love with you! And she will never forgive herself for what happened, a woman like that, so maternal. Although no woman gets over it. I should know."

"What are you talking about?"

"You've never asked me why I have no children."

Ned was taken aback by the bitterness in her voice. "Because it was obvious. You had a singing career and children would have interfered with it."

"Some people have both."

"Precious few."

"But I had no choice."

"Why are you being so enigmatic? The exotic Hungarian routine doesn't impress me anymore, Magda. Just tell me what you mean."

Magda took a long drag of her cigarette, then blew the smoke out slowly as she ground the stub round and round in a crystal ashtray. Finally, without meeting his eyes, she spoke.

"I too had an abortion. When I was quite young, I fell in love with a much older man, a conductor, married, famous — you would probably recognize his name. He paid for the procedure, he said he knew somebody reliable, but there were complications. Very bad ones. And then I could not have children afterwards. You have no idea how I've suffered."

Ned did not know what to say. A sudden crash of metal on metal from the kitchen bought him extra time to think of a response, but his mind just gaped; probably his mouth did too. Everyone had secrets. Even Magda, whom he'd thought invulnerable, had her own portion of unspeakable sorrow.

"But why didn't you tell me, Magda?"

"This is not something you tell people. Even Stefan doesn't know. Luckily, he never wanted children. That was one of the reasons I married him."

"So what are you saying? That I should have had a child I didn't want?"

"Maybe we don't always want what is best for us."

"You don't really believe that!"

"I don't know what I believe anymore. This is not the world I thought I knew. But maybe I never knew it, maybe I never knew anything."

They sat in silence for a moment. Ned covered her hand with his. It felt small and cold.

"Things don't always work out the way we plan, Edward. Who knows how my life would have been if I had refused that abortion? Who knows how your life would have been if you had married Clara and had the baby?"

"Oh, please, Magda, I couldn't. You know that."

"Yes, unfortunately, I know that."

Jacob practised his bar mitzvah portion diligently, if without much enthusiasm. He didn't really enjoy singing the ancient tropes because they were so limited. The human voice was capable of more range than this nasal sliding up and down a minor key. King David had appointed four thousand Levites as court musicians, so obviously there was a time when Jewish music was worth listening to. But since the destruction of the second Temple, instruments had been banished from Jewish worship. All those mentioned in the Torah — the hazozra, the kinnor, the ugav, the tof — were lost. And this unaccompanied wailing was all that remained.

Jews were always in mourning it seemed. Like him, since his father died. When he asked why Papa had to get sick, Zayde always replied that God's ways were mysterious. But Jacob was beginning to wonder whether these really were God's ways. Maybe God too was in exile or on permanent vacation, his hand withdrawn from a world of inexplicable absences.

Like Dr. Abraham's. Jacob wanted to talk to him about the scholarship mess. He wanted to talk to him about Zayde moving into his room and the way the old man prayed interminably before he went to bed and then whimpered and cried out in his sleep. He even wanted to talk to him about being jealous of Evvie's newly discovered musical talent. Things were changing too fast. He no longer knew who he was or what he wanted, and Dr. Abraham was the only one who would understand. Even his friend Nathaniel was no use. He knew exactly who he was and where he was going; he was his father's son, following in his father's footsteps. Talking to Nathaniel just made Jacob lonelier than ever.

So he'd called Dr. Abraham's office, despite his mother's admonition not to pester the man, but no one answered. He'd inquired at the Guildhall, but no one had seen him there in more than a month. He'd even asked Miss Westerham, but she knew nothing either.

"Did you want to work on another piece with him, Jacob?"

"Well, maybe. If he does. The thing is . . . I need to talk to him. You know, about my sister taking up the violin. And other things."

"Of course. It's natural for you to want to talk to a man sometimes," said Miss Westerham, trying to ignore the pinch of jealousy in her diaphragm, reminding herself that she'd brought the two of them together in the first place.

"Would you like me to call him for you?"

"Oh, would you? Thanks a lot! I asked Mum, but she said it wouldn't be right to bother him because he's always so busy. But I'm sure he wouldn't mind. He told me I could call him if I ever needed anything."

For the next week Jacob waited in great excitement for the doctor's call, but it never came. And at his next piano lesson, Miss Westerham greeted him with an unusually solemn face.

"Jacob, I'm afraid I have some rather disturbing news," she said.

"About Dr. Abraham?"

"Yes, about Dr. Abraham."

"Is he all right? I mean, where is he, anyway?"

"Well, that's just it. No one seems to know."

"What do you mean no one knows?"

"His mother is staying with his sister, and they haven't heard from him in weeks. She's frantic, poor dear. Apparently he went to Vienna for a month, and then he set out on some kind of mountain-climbing expedition in the Alps. Silly thing to do, if you ask me, risking life and limb like that. Anyhow, he sent her an address in the mountains where he said he would be picking up his post, but he never showed up there, and his friends in Vienna haven't heard from him either since he left."

"But people don't just disappear, do they? Maybe he changed his mind and forgot to tell her, or maybe his letters got lost. I once got an invitation to a party a whole week late. If it can take two weeks for a letter to get across London, it must take a lot longer from Vienna, mustn't it?"

"Of course. I'm sure you're right, Jacob," Miss Westerham said, trying to sound calmer than she felt. This was all her fault, for meddling. For trying to cheer Jacob up by finding a father figure for him. She'd never forgive herself. Why had she been so stupid, so interfering, such a bossy, interfering old maid? Why do we always think other people's problems are easier to solve than our own? She'd made life immeasurably worse for Jacob by making him suffer yet another loss.

"At any rate, I've asked Mrs. Abraham to ring me as soon

as she hears something, and then I'll call you right away, I promise. I'm sorry, Jacob, really I am. I know how fond of each other you were."

"No, you don't! Nobody does. All anyone else cares about is my stupid music. He was the only one who cared about *me*."

"Oh, Jacob, I care about you very much, I always have. You know that, don't you?"

"It's not the same. You're my teacher. He was my friend."

"I would like to be your friend too, if you'd let me."

"I still want Dr. Abraham. I need him."

"Yes, of course you do. I understand, Jacob." And with that, Miss Westerham gathered the boy into her arms, something she'd never dared to do before, and wondered at the passion shaking those narrow shoulders. How could she ever make up for what she'd done?

Clara started painting again. She set up an easel in the sitting room right by the window and bought nice fat tubes of paint and soft sable brushes. She cleaned up her old palette and knife, rejoicing in the smell of turpentine that pervaded the house. Evvie and Danny liked this new, busy Clara, for she was home with them a lot now. Sometimes they would sit by her with their own muddy watercolours and stiff, shedding brushes, working on the same project. "Let's paint something angry," she would say. "What colour would that be?" Or "Let's all paint a happy dream. Who can remember a good one?"

Danny specialized in monsters with multiple arms and

spiky hair. He tended to use one colour at a time, generally red. Evvie favoured landscapes with stylized trees and tulips, smiling suns, symmetrical rainbows, and puffy white clouds. Often a mother and daughter strolled through the landscape, hand in hand, wearing matching frocks and hair ribbons. Occasionally a brother or two was allowed to wander onto the scene, but the brothers were always smaller than the other two figures and considerably duller.

Today they had attempted a still life: red roses, white daisies, blue vase, yellow tablecloth. The children had finished long ago and run off to have tea with Millie in the garden. Clara could hear shrieks of laughter as they ran through the wet grass; she reckoned she had about fifteen minutes before somebody got hurt and they all came trooping in to demand her attention, screaming he pushed me first, and it wasn't my fault, I tripped. She had better make the most of it and work as fast as possible.

White was always the hardest to get right. She'd tried different techniques. Sometimes she took the easiest route, caging the luminous flowers in a heavy black outline. Other times she made it an exercise in abstraction, working from the background forward, delineating form by the absence of colour, a white blur on green. And yet again, she could parse pallor: cream, peach, lavender, fawn, grey. Pale blue. Pale green. A pale shadow of the real blooms. But nothing satisfied her.

She could cheat, of course, just pull the daisies out of the bouquet and do a better job of the roses on their own. But roses were too sentimental, too full of easy poetry; she needed the homely astringency of daisies to balance them. Or something else austere and harsh, anything might do. And without thinking, Clara smashed the milk jug and spilled the flowers onto the table, where they lay in the silent aftermath of disaster, their beauty compromised but her composition much enhanced.

She had never thought of herself as someone who smashed things. She had always been the good daughter, the good wife, the good mother. She made wholesome meals and her garden was the envy of the neighbourhood. Had it all been a lie, all those years of trying to please other people? Deep down she was wicked and vengeful, as much a destroyer as Ned himself. But how could he have gone to Austria knowing full well everything that was going on there? Was he utterly mad?

She'd never forgive herself if anything bad happened to him. She had only wanted to hurt him as he'd hurt her, to make him feel helpless and manipulated and of no account. But she hadn't wanted to endanger him in any way. Please, please, don't let him be hurt, she prayed. Whatever God there is, take care of him, and forgive me.

Clara tore the sheet off her easel and began again, sketching in the jagged pieces of pottery and the torn flowers. Was it a portrait of Ned, or of herself?

Sunlight swirled around him, a split prism. So high! And higher still, the Alps were capped with snow: permanent white, unreachable, unchanging. He'd come through a wet layer of cloud and now looked through it as though it were sea foam, swirling around those jagged black crags below. So there were really two oceans, one of sky and one of sea. That made sense, since islands were really mountain peaks soaring from the ocean floor. Continents were the same, if one thought about them properly. If one thought about anything, however vast, it echoed something smaller and then something smaller still, like reflections back and forth in a pair of mirrors. And the reverse too: an endless chain of patterns, all logically related, the way Bach reworked a motif in a fugue.

Ned's heart hammered loudly and his legs trembled with fatigue. The occasional tramp across the Hackney Marshes was no training for an adventure like this. Nonetheless, he felt he'd been preparing for this climb all his life. England seemed so far away, with all the muddle and misery of the last few months. The only token of that bungled past was his violin, bumping against his back in its clumsy case. Don't worry, my love, he thought. I haven't forgotten you.

He decided to take a rest and play a little music, but the cold and damp had soured his strings. As he tuned them, Ned watched an eagle glide upward on a thermal, effortlessly, its wingspread the height of a man. His music would be like that today, though there was no one to hear him — no one but a mother goat and her kid, browsing moss on an adjacent ledge, eyeing him and his instrument suspiciously, ready to flee. How steady they were on those slender legs, and how precipitous the drop beneath them! If other creatures could thrive in a place as remote and inhospitable as this, there must be a home for him somewhere on the earth.

Vienna hadn't been as welcoming as he'd hoped; Magda was right about that, though he hadn't told her so. As soon as this mountain-climbing expedition was over, he must find another sanctuary. Though he'd tried to make London his home, learning the history of each bridge and monument, walking countless miles along its rivers, he had never really belonged there. But where should he go?

Well, for the moment he was here, and there was no point

thinking about anything else. He lifted his violin and began to play. Above him, the snow began to hiss and murmur, like an audience whispering approval around a concert hall. Then the applause grew and grew; it became thunderous; it gathered speed and strength and hurled itself down on him in a fury of white. Out of the corner of his eye he saw a man in the flapping cloak of a Russian peddler beckoning to him. He opened his mouth to call "Father!" and let the silence in.

Coda

"In May 1939 an International Conference was held in London. It was perhaps the last successful international effort before the outbreak of war. France, Germany, Great Britain, Holland, and Italy were represented, and memoranda were sent in by Switzerland and by the United States of America. The conference unanimously adopted '440 cycles per second for the note A in the treble clef.'"

Alexander Wood,
The Physics of Music

Acknowledgements

This book was inspired by the life of my great-great-uncle, Dr. Samuel Nagley, who disappeared while climbing in the Austrian Alps after losing his medical license for performing an abortion on his (never-married, childless) mistress. The archivists of the General Medical Council in London were able to track down his records, though they could shed little light on his case. For that I had to go to Anna Wyner and Harold Caplan, who shared the family's only memories of Uncle Sam. Harold gave me the hand-written score of Sam's fugue for violin, cello, and piano, which is the inspiration for the book's closing chapter, and Anna gave me his photograph, let me stay with her to do research, read successive drafts, and patiently corrected my abysmal spelling.

For sharing their musical expertise, my thanks go to John Desmond Black, Miriam Katzin, and Jan Zwicky. I learned a great deal from CBC Radio Two and from reading David Burrows, *Sound, Speech, and Music*; Robert Jourdain, *Music, the Brain, and Ecstasy: How Music Captures our Imagination*; Yehudi Menuhin, *Life Class: Thoughts, Exercises, Reflections of an Itinerant Violinist*; Charles Rosen, *Sonata Forms*; R.

Murray Schafer, *The Tuning of the World*; and Alexander Wood, *The Physics of Music*.

My understanding of Jewish history in Britain is indebted to Chaim Bermant, *Troubled Eden: An Anatomy of British Jewry*; Lloyd Gartner, *The Jewish Immigrant in England, 1870-1914*; Ernest Krausz, *Leeds Jewry: Its History and Structure*; Emanuel Litvinoff, *Journey through a Small Planet*; and Barbara Tuchman, *Bible and Sword: England and Palestine from the Bronze Age to Balfour*.

Special thanks to special friends for their encouragement, particularly Martha Baillie and Michael Redhill for generous editorial advice, Helen Dunmore for being a continuing inspiration, and Mary di Michele, Susan Free, Eden Graber, Carolyn Smart, and the late Sheldon Zitner for reading and commenting along the way. For making this book as good as it could be, I am grateful to everyone at Goose Lane Editions: Susanne Alexander, Julie Scriver, Lisa Alward, and especially Laurel Boone, editor nonpareil. And to my husband, Toan Klein, and our children, Jesse and Rachel, thank you for everything, always.